Blood and Ink

Stephen Davies

Charlesbridge
TEEN

2017 First US Edition
Text copyright © 2017 by Stephen Davies
Jacket illustration © 2017 by Blake Morrow

Published by Charlesbridge
85 Main Street
Watertown, MA 02472
(617) 926-0329
www.charlesbridge.com

First published in 2015 by
Andersen Press Limited
20 Vauxhall Bridge Road
London SW1V 2SA
www.andersenpress.co.uk

Library of Congress Cataloging-in-Publication Data

Names: Davies, Stephen, 1976– author.
Title: Blood and ink / Stephen Davies.
Description: First US edition. | Watertown, MA : Charlesbridge, 2017. |
"First published in 2015 by Andersen Press Limited . . . London"—Copyright page. |
Summary: Kadija is the music-loving daughter of a guardian of the library in the ancient
city of Timbuktu, Ali is a former shepherd boy, trained by Islamist militants—and both
are caught up in the war in Mali and on opposite sides of the struggle to save the sacred
Sufi manuscripts that the militants want to destroy.
Identifiers: LCCN 2016009434 I ISBN 9781580897907 (reinforced for library use)
Subjects: LCSH: Islamic fundamentalism—Juvenile fiction. | Terrorists—Juvenile fiction. |
Islamic antiquities—Juvenile fiction. | Sufi literature—Juvenile fiction. | Sufism—Mali—
Juvenile fiction. | Tombouctou (Mali)—Politics and government—21st century—
Juvenile fiction. | Mali—History—Tuareg Rebellion, 2012—Juvenile fiction. | CYAC:
Islamic fundamentalism—Fiction. | Terrorism—Fiction. | Antiquities—Fiction. | Sufism—
Mali—Fiction. | Tombouctou (Mali)—Fiction. | Mali—History—Tuareg Rebellion,
2012—Fiction. | LCGFT: Thrillers (Fiction)
Classification: [LCC PZ7.D2845 Bl 2017 | DDC 823.92 [Fic] —dc23 LC record
available at https://lccn.loc.gov/2016009434

Printed in the United States of America
(hc) 10 9 8 7 6 5 4 3 2 1

Display type set in ArabDances
Text type set in Adobe Garamond Pro
Printed by Berryville Graphics in Berryville, Virginia, USA
Color separations by Coral Graphic Services, Inc. in Hicksville, New York, USA
Production supervision by Brian G. Walker
Designed by Susan Mallory Sherman

For Debbie and Sven, with love

MAURITANIA

GUINEA

Bamako

Niger

Mop

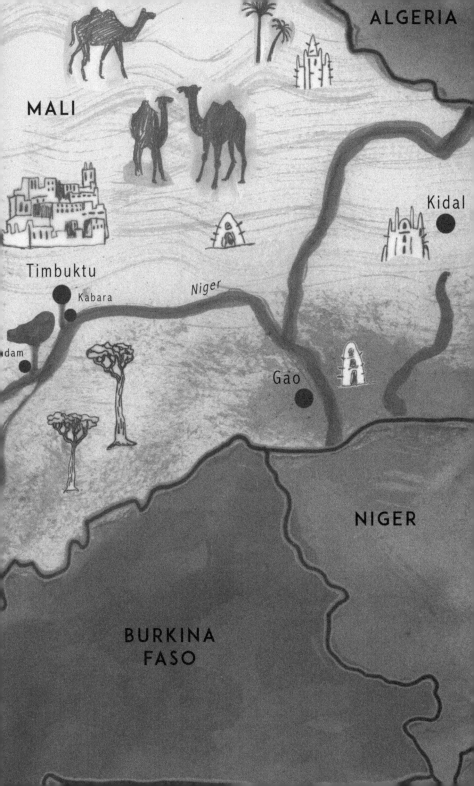

ALGERIA

MALI

Kidal

Timbuktu

Kabara

Niger

dam

Gao

NIGER

BURKINA
FASO

Blood and Ink

Glossary

balaphone (Manding) a West African percussion instrument; an ancestor of the xylophone

baraka (Arabic) blessing

dhikr (Arabic) reciting a series of short phrases in praise of God

djembe (Manding) a West African drum made from hardwood and goatskin

djinn (Arabic) spirit beings in Islam; can be benevolent or mischievous

haram (Arabic) forbidden by Islamic law

hijab (Arabic) a veil that covers the head and chest; worn by many Muslim women

jihad (Arabic) holy struggle; often seen as a call to arms

kora (Manding) a West African harp-lute with twenty-one strings

marabout (French from Arabic) a teacher of Islam

mujahid (plural: mujahidin) (Arabic) warrior

ngoni (Manding) a West African guitar with four strings; an ancestor of the banjo

qadi (Arabic) judge

Qur'an (Arabic) Islam's main religious text, which Muslims believe to be a revelation from God

sharia (Arabic) Islamic law

Sufism (Arabic) a mystical branch of Islam

Sura (Arabic) a chapter of the Qur'an

tarikh (Arabic) a history or chronicle

timbakewen (Tamasheq) those who guard objects

Ali

I lie on my front on the crest of the dune. The sand is hot against my chest, the goatskin satchel tight against my shoulders. I take a deep breath and pull a fold of my turban up over my nose and mouth. The newly washed fabric smells sweet, like victory.

"Are you filming?"

Omar holds up my phone and presses a button. "Now I am."

My mission is simple.

Descend the dune. Cross the wadi. Scale the wall. Smite the enemy.

"Go with God, Ali," whispers Omar in my ear. "Think of your namesake at the Battle of Badr."

I stand up and sprint down the dune, the sand sliding away beneath me. *Lion of God with the strength of God. There is no one like Ali, and there is no sword like Zulfiqaar.* Fast and light on the balls of my feet, I skitter sideways down the slope, all the way to the bottom. The dry riverbed lies before me, a jagged scar bisecting the desert. I speed up, shorten my stride, and leap.

1

Reach with the arms, pedal with the legs, land with a roll.
Perfect.

The next challenge is the wall. I drop into a crouch and reach over my shoulder into the goatskin satchel. *Cord in the left hand. Claw in the right. Eyes on the parapet.*

Five years of shepherding in the desert is good training for a warrior of God. If you can protect your sheep, you can protect your brothers. If you can master yourself, you can master an enemy. If you can kill the lion that threatens your flock, you can kill an infidel. If you can make your staff fly high and straight to knock down a baobab fruit, you can make a metal claw fly high and straight as well.

I take a deep breath and feel its weight in my right hand. Then I swing my arm and let it fly.

Up it floats, and hooks itself neatly over the top of the wall, as I knew it must. *Alhamdulillah!*

With my hands on the rope and my bare feet pressing against the hot concrete bricks, I climb. A mujahid is weightless. He is all spirit. With God's help he can scale a high wall in a second.

At the top I reach over my shoulder and take out a second length of rope. I tie it to the hook, and rappel down the far side of the wall.

I have breached the defenses of the camp. On my right, two large termite mounds stand on guard. On my left, two sacks of bambara beans sleep deeply. I reach over my shoulder one last time and draw from my satchel a pistol and a hand grenade.

Call on Ali, who is able to bring about the extraordinary. O Ali! O Ali! O Ali!

I line up the pistol sights and fire two bullets into the bean sacks. Then I pull the grenade pin with my teeth and lob the deadly fruit toward the termite mounds.

BOOM.

The rock quakes under my feet. Fragments of termite mound descend like rain. The enemies of God have been vanquished.

"God is great!" cries Redbeard, striding into view around the side of the wall. He claps his leathery hands and a grin spreads all over his desert-hardened face. Behind him come Omar, Rashid, Hilal, Hamza, and the rest of the Brothers. Omar's eyes behind his thick glasses look bigger than ever. He is still filming.

"Forty-five seconds!" declares Redbeard, holding up his watch. "You, Ali, are my champion infiltrator."

"Thank you, master."

"Behold the infidels," chuckles Redbeard, bending over the bambara-bean sacks and slipping a finger into one of the bullet holes. "I don't suppose this one will ever eat pork again."

We laugh obediently.

When Redbeard straightens up, the smile is gone. "Tell me, Ali Konana, could you do it if the wall were a little higher? Could you hook it?"

"*Inshallah*, master. God willing."

"What if it were night, with only half a moon?"

"Yes, master. With God's help, I could."

☾

After infiltration practice comes target practice.

The fisherboys Hilal and Hamza shinny up the rope onto the top of the wall and edge their way along the parapet, setting empty tomato paste cans at equal distances. The rest of us fetch our weapons from the back of a donkey cart. My AK-47 is marked with the same lopsided cross I used to use for my cows. We sling the guns across our bodies and follow Redbeard across the shimmering sand toward a distant dune, no longer a ragtag group of teenagers but a proud, invincible battalion.

"Who can tell me," says Redbeard, "why the AK-47 is the greatest gun in the world?"

"I know, master," gasps Omar, his fingertips reaching for the sun. "I know, I know."

"Go on."

"Easy to strip, easy to clean, easy to fire," chants Omar. "Spits out seven hundred rounds a minute. Never overheats or jams, not even in a sandstorm. A child can use it."

"Even my little brother can use it," whispers Hilal, "and he's not much bigger than his gun!"

Hamza stares straight ahead, pretending not to have heard, but his nostrils twitch like they always do when he is angry. The fisherboys are twins, but they are not identical. Not even similar, in fact. Hilal is tall and Hamza short. Hilal is the comedian of the group and Hamza the thundercloud.

We trudge up the side of the dune and line up along the crest.

"Thirty rounds each on full auto," barks Redbeard. "Go."

We shoulder our guns and one by one we rattle off our rounds. Hamza is the best marksman of us all—five tins in four deafening seconds.

By the time it gets to be my turn, there are no cans left on the wall, so Redbeard tells me to pick out a brick instead. I kick off my sandals, rest my finger on the trigger, and fire.

In four joyous, bone-rattling seconds, my chosen brick and several of its neighbors dissolve to dust.

The other boys take their turns. We only built this wall yesterday, and now it looks like one of Hamza's fishing nets.

Redbeard goes last. With his thirty rounds, he strobes the weakened areas of the wall and reduces the entire edifice to a pile of rubble. Some of the boys whoop and slap each other on the back.

"Incredible," I gasp.

"I know," Omar whispers. "They say he once shot down an Algerian helicopter with that rifle."

The cheering and clapping die down, and now there is another noise, an eerie rumbling sound that swells to a boom and then to a roar. It sounds like the voice of God himself.

Redbeard puts down his gun and stretches out his arms. "The desert is singing!" he cries. "Who can tell me why the desert is singing?"

"Our shooting disturbed the dune," gabbles Omar, forgetting to raise his hand. "Billions of sand grains are sliding away from the crest, each layer of sand rubbing against the one beneath it like a bow against a violin. You can't see the sandslide but you can hear the—"

"Nonsense!" cries Redbeard. "It is joy that makes the desert sing. She hears the gunfire of the mujahidin and she knows that a new day of faith and justice is about to dawn."

He glares around him, as if daring anyone to contradict him. No one does.

☾

Lunch is rice and bambara beans, as usual. We crouch in the shade, five boys to a bowl. Going sunwise around the circle, we take it in turns to palm a clump of rice and beans and raise it to our mouths.

Hilal says these beans are from the sack I shot this morning. After every mouthful, he clutches his throat and rolls his eyes in their sockets, pretending to choke on a bullet. The other boys are laughing like hyenas, which only encourages him.

"Peace be upon you," says a voice behind us.

5

Hamza.

"Brother, join us!" says Hilal. "Sit down, if you haven't already. I'm never quite sure."

General cackling from the group.

"I have a message for you," mutters Hamza.

"Give it," says Hilal. "I like messages."

The stocky fisherboy grabs his brother by the hair and knees him in the face. "Stop mocking me," he says.

☾

After two o'clock prayers we recite the Qur'an in unison. The name of today's chapter is Al-Anfal. *And you did not kill them, but it was God who killed them. And you threw not, when you threw, but it was God who threw that He might test the believers with a good test.*

Omar and I learned our Arabic with a marabout back home in Goundam. On winter evenings we huddled round the fire in his courtyard, twelve small boys with furrowed foreheads and flapping tongues, writing and reciting long into the night. The firewood never used to last very long. In the early hours of the morning the embers glowed dim and the breeze from the Niger River made us cringe and shiver. The marabout was never cold, of course. Shrouded in a thick cotton blanket, he emerged only to correct our pronunciation or to scold us that our ink was too watery. He never talked about the Qur'an itself or told us how these peculiar Arabic verses might be relevant to our lives. However many hours we studied, our hearts remained as cold and numb as the fingers that clasped our writing boards.

This training camp is not like that. Here the fierce sun warms our bodies and the words of the Book warm our hearts. We learn about the prophets, peace be upon them, shepherds just like us. The Prophet Ibrahim, the father of nations, loved to fill his eyes with sheep and goats. The Prophet Musa walked behind a flock for forty years before God sent him to challenge Pharaoh. The Prophet Daouda chanted God's praises with a shepherd's crook in one hand and a slingshot in the other.

The last of the prophets was the Prophet Muhammad, peace be upon him, the shepherd who became a warrior. We learn about his nights of solitude and prayer on Mount Hira, his visit from the angel Jibreel, his zeal to prove to the world that there is no god but God. We learn about his friends—Omar, Bilal, Jabir, Hilal, Rashid, Iyas, Hamza—courageous in the cause of God and utterly devoted to their leader. We learn about Ali, bravest of the lot, the Lion of God with the strength of God. Wielding his shining scimitar, Zulfiqaar, he protected his master in the thick of battle.

When we first arrived at the camp three months ago, Redbeard gave us new names. He named us after the Prophet's companions in the hope that we might acquire their bravery and devotion.

In our camp, there is no memorization without understanding, no recitation without conviction. Redbeard leads us in discussion and each boy gets to speak. We talk of God and Satan, angels and djinn, presidents and paupers, heroes and villains. We talk of battles to be won against disbelief, against the desires of the flesh, and against the Malian army.

Those who disbelieved devised plans against you, plans to confine you or slay you or drive you away; they devised their plans, but God also had arranged a plan; and God is the best of planners!

As we recite those holy words, I realize that I am shivering—not with cold but with excitement.

༄

After recitation, Redbeard makes an announcement.

"I just received a telephone call, boys. Gao has fallen! The Tuaregs invaded this morning, along with one of our Al Qaeda battalions, and already they are in full control."

A cheer goes up. Hilal whips off his turban and throws it in the air.

"Kidal and Gao are ours," says Redbeard. "Timbuktu is next. When Timbuktu falls, we will rule the whole Sahara. We will return the desert peoples to the worship of the one true God—and after the desert, the entire world, from where the sun rises to where it sets!"

My spirit leaps. Someone in the row behind slaps me on the back. This is a golden moment.

"Be warned," says Redbeard. "Timbuktu is not like those other towns. The army garrison is strong and they are expecting our invasion. We must be cunning, like serpents."

A murmur of excitement thrills through the ranks. If our master needs cunning, so be it. We will give whatever he asks, and more.

"As soon as darkness falls," says Redbeard, "Alhassan Litni will meet us here with one hundred and fifty of his best fighting men. As you know, Litni is a Tuareg chief and a courageous warrior. In the last ten years he has fought many battles against the Malian army and has inflicted heavy losses. I have allowed him the honor of commanding this operation."

I feel a pang of disappointment. I thought Redbeard himself would lead us into battle, not that crafty camelman Alhassan Litni.

"Litni will lead you well," continues Redbeard, "but there is one thing that he and his men lack."

"Soap," I mutter.

"No!" Redbeard glares at me, and for one heady moment I think he is going to strike me. "What Litni's battalion lacks is

8

stealth. If we are to have the advantage of surprise, I need ten of you boys to spearhead a silent invasion. The boys I choose must be invisible, inaudible and deadly—like djinn."

Already there are hands in the air, pleading hands thrust up so high that every sinew strains. My hand shoots up as well, propelled by God himself.

"They must be strong of limb, fleet of foot, utterly devoted to God and to our cause. They must be ready to kill—and to be killed."

Omar's hand goes up as well. There is not a single boy in this battalion who does not long for the glory of martyrdom.

"As I said, ten of you will suffice. I choose"—his pointing finger slices through the air—"Hilal, Hamza, Rashid, Malik, Bilal, Usman, Zayd, Jabir, Omar, and Ali Konana."

I want to leap in the air and shout for joy, but that would be shameful. I just nod instead.

"Ali, you will do for real tonight what you have done today in practice. You will infiltrate the city at dead of night, scale the wall of the Sidi el Beckaye Fort, and lead the attack inside the enemy's camp."

Tonight. Yes, of course. I have seen it in my dreams.

"There will be sentries," warns Redbeard. "Not termite mounds and sacks of beans, but living, breathing, beer-swilling infidels with assault rifles. Take no chances, Ali. If a sentry sees you, open fire. Otherwise, wait for the rest of your platoon to climb up and join you. Wait as long as possible before engaging the enemy. Keep your nerve. Surprise is on your side. Ali, Hilal, Hamza, Rashid, Jabir, you will rappel down to the ground, fight your way across the compound, and open the gates for Litni and his men. Malik, Bilal, Usman, Zayd, and Omar, you will stay on top of the wall and lay down covering fire.

"Once the military camp is ours, you will split up and follow Litni's men to the radio station, the police station, and the airport. I expect little or no resistance at these sites. By noon tomorrow, Timbuktu will be ours.

"Go with God, boys. Watch your brothers' backs, and show the enemy no mercy. Peace be upon you."

Manuscript 8,467: the tarikh of Sidi Ahmed ben Amar

Sidi Ahmed ben Amar was one of the holy men of Timbuktu. He was a teacher at the Sankore Mosque, well known for his love of God and his gentle spirit. He had many disciples and they all adored him.

One day, ben Amar accepted a loan from a one-eyed Berabish merchant, promising to pay him back in forty days when his salt caravan came in from the desert. Forty days came and went, and still ben Amar's salt caravan had not arrived. The merchant went to see ben Amar and shook his fist in the saint's face. "Pay me what you owe me!" he cried.

"Be patient, friend," said the saint. "A man makes plans in his heart, but his destiny is in the hands of God. Allow me three more days to pay my debt."

"Twenty-four hours," said the Berabish, and off he went.

Sidi Ahmed ben Amar went straight to see the chief of Timbuktu and announced to him that God's power would visit Timbuktu that night. The chief told the minstrel, and the minstrel marched around town with a big drum. He warned everyone to stay indoors, for a miracle was on its way.

That night Sidi Ahmed ben Amar went out into his courtyard and spread out his prayer skin under the stars. He closed his eyes, leaned forward, and began to pray. What happened next is sung about to this day in every nomad camp in the Sahara desert.

A huge slab of salt fell from the sky. It landed next to the spot where ben Amar was praying, one big slab and then another.

That's right, slabs of salt from the sky.

Ben Amar prayed for many hours. Salt fell all around him and a great wind battered the roofs of Timbuktu. People cowered in their houses, gnashing their teeth and begging Allah for mercy.

The slabs of salt fell so hard and fast that his compound became a vast crater, yet still ben Amar prayed. At three o'clock in the morning, Halimatu, the saint's third wife, stripped off her clothing and ran outside. She clambered across the slabs of salt to where her husband knelt, and snatched the prayer beads from his hands.

"Stop it!" cried Halimatu. "You'll kill us all! Stop it!"

The sight of his naked wife distracted ben Amar from his prayers, and the salt stopped falling.

For many months after the miracle, no one in Timbuktu paid money for cooking salt or cattle licks. They gathered it free of charge in the yard of Sidi Ahmed ben Amar. Even the one-eyed merchant went along to beg the saint's forgiveness—and for some salt.

Today there is a crater behind the Sankore Mosque where Sidi Ahmed's salt slabs landed. It is called the crater of Takaboundou. Ben Amar's tomb stands in the Cemetery of the Three to the southwest of Timbuktu, and people come from all over Africa to visit the shrine and ask for things they need. They do a special, whirling dance and they sing these words:

> *We entreat your blessing, Sidi Ahmed ben Amar,*
> *Son of Sidi el Wafi, son of Sidi el Moctar,*
> *For daily salt we beg thee, Sidi Ahmed ben Amar,*
> *Let the heavens rain down on us.*

Kadija

The afternoon is crazy hot, and tempers in the club are fraying.

"Come on, girl, this is a wedding we're preparing for, not a rally," says Alpha, pointing a balaphone mallet straight at me. "Let's have none of your political songs."

I am with the band at the La Détente nightclub in Timbuktu, rehearsing music for my friend Tondi's wedding party in two weeks' time. We perch on stools upon that hallowed stage where so many of Mali's greats have plucked and strummed and sung their way to glory: King of the Blues Ali Farka Touré, Salif "Golden Voice" Keita, Kandia "La Dangereuse" Kouyaté. One day, perhaps, our names will be spoken along with theirs and our photos will join theirs on the walls of La Détente. But only if we don't kill each other first.

"'Alla La Ke' is not a political song," I tell him. "It's a song for peace. It's a heart cry for our country."

Our country. Over the last few years, a terrible shadow has overtaken us. Our radios relay news of kidnappings, uprisings, and assassinations. They talk of dark forces massing in the desert, preparing to attack, and now, since last week's coup, the fear is at an all-time high. My father says that Al Qaeda and the Tuaregs are working together now. They have control of Kidal, but they won't stop there. They'll march on Gao—and then on Timbuktu.

"We don't do political songs," repeats Alpha, staring me down with his sightless eyes.

"It's not political!" I stab my finger in the air, not that Alpha can see it. "If a bird sees a woodcutter coming to chop down the tree that holds her nest, and she squawks to alert her family, do you call that political?"

"Definitely," he says.

"You just don't want to admit you're wrong," I snap. "What about you, Yusuf? If you and me go swimming naked in the Great River and a crocodile gets hold of me and you shout out to raise the alarm, is that political?"

Yusuf's pupils dilate and his fingertips tighten on the strings of his ngoni. "We've never done that," he mutters, and the others burst out laughing.

"We're doing the song," I tell them flatly. "I'm the leader of this group, and I say we're doing the song."

༄

I walk home with Aisha after band practice, and the millet pounders all around us put rhythm in our step. *POK-POK, POK-POK, POK-POK-POK*, we bob along together in the rosy afternoon.

"You're cruel to flirt with Yusuf," says Aisha, taking my hand. "You know he's mad about you."

"It's not flirting," I say. "If you were Fulani, you would understand. It's normal for Fulani to tease their cousins."

"And marry them too," she says. "Do you love Yusuf?"

14

"Only when he's playing the ngoni. When he stops playing, I stop loving him."

"Well then," she says, "stop giving him false hope."

We pass the Well of Old Buktu and take a shortcut through the market. The sun is so fierce at this time of year, it burns your brain. When I shut my eyes, I see market stalls outlined in blue and pink on the insides of my eyelids.

"I like giving him false hope," I say. "It makes me feel powerful."

Aisha looks at me sharply, and I manage to keep a straight face for all of two seconds before I burst out laughing.

"Girls, come here!" a woman calls. "I've got something for you."

It's Mama's friend Halimatu Tal, frying bite-size millet pancakes over a fire. She puts four pancakes in a plastic bag and hands the bag to me.

"Thank you, Auntie," I say, and curtsy.

At the exit to the market, an old woman is bargaining with a merchant for a sack of rice.

"Forty thousand francs," the merchant tells her.

"You're killing me," says the woman. "It was thirty last week."

"And now it's forty," says the merchant, unmoved.

"Crazy," I mutter as we walk on past. "Only the mayor's wife can afford to eat rice at forty thousand a sack."

"If you want a sack of rice, you should go and sing 'Alla La Ke' outside the mayor's gate," says Aisha. "I hear he likes political songs."

I push her into a passing donkey and she squeals with laughter.

We leave the market by the west gate and amble down Toumani Avenue toward Independence Square. As we pass in front of the Sidi Yahya Mosque, my father phones me.

"Come home quick," he says. "Gao has fallen to the rebels."

☾

Timbuktu is a slow town, especially in the hot season. People saunter. If they are late for something, they stroll. But as the news about Gao spreads from tongue to tongue around Independence Square, there is striding and even some scurrying. If Gao has fallen, Timbuktu is next.

I can't believe they've invaded Gao so fast. My father thought it would take weeks, but it's happened in two days.

I say goodbye to Aisha and cross the square alone. In the middle of the square stands a statue of Al Farouk, the great protector djinni of Timbuktu. "Good luck, Al Farouk," I murmur as I pass. "You've got some work to do."

I turn right up Askia Street and then duck through a mud-brick archway into our family's compound.

Marimba is licking a slab of salt in his trough. When he hears the creak of his gate, he looks up and whinnies at me.

"Stay away," I tell him. "I still haven't forgiven you for what you did to me."

It was more than ten years ago that Marimba kicked me, but I've never ridden since. If a thing is dangerous, don't mess with it, that's what I say.

Ignoring Marimba's liquid gaze, I skirt round the edge of the horse enclosure and slip into a narrow gap behind the hay bales. In the darkness I feel along the wall until I find what I am looking for, an ancient wooden door with silver rivets.

Only eight living creatures know about this door—seven humans and one horse.

I open the door silently and tiptoe down the mud-brick steps. Ever since I was small I have loved the earthy, papery smell of this secret vault. The smell of wisdom, Baba calls it.

A paraffin lamp on a table casts an eerie orange glow across the walls of the underground chamber. The table, a chair, and a closed bookcase are the only furniture, and the only decoration is a seventeenth-century Kabyle musket hanging on the staircase wall. Its wooden stock is skillfully inlaid with swirls of ivory, and the silver lock plate gleams.

My father is taking manuscripts off bookshelves and stuffing them into metal trunks. His back is turned and he jumps when he feels my hand on his shoulder.

"Kadija, don't creep up on me like that."

"Another power cut, Baba?"

"I'm afraid so." Lit from beneath by the paraffin lamp, his face looks wan and hollow-cheeked.

"Are you moving them out of the vault, Baba?"

"No, I'm simply making them more portable. I do not believe the rebels will take Timbuktu. Our army garrison will be too strong for them."

"You said the same about Kidal and Gao."

"That proves it." He smiles. "I'm never wrong three times in a row. Now stop prattling, girl, and get to work. I want you to log these manuscripts for me."

I sit down at the table and pull the notebook and pencil toward me. "April 2012" reads the Arabic script on the cover. "New manuscript locations."

"Stories of the saints," says Baba, taking a manuscript out of the cabinet. "The tarikh of Sidi Ahmed ben Amar." He lays it in the trunk.

"Sidi Ahmed ben Amar," I repeat, writing in the book. "Trunk thirty-two."

He gathers up another manuscript. "The tarikh of Sidi Yahya."

"Sidi Yahya."

"The tarikh of Muhammad Fodiri Al-Wangari."

17

"Al-Wangari."

"The tarikh of Sidi el Beckaye."

"El Beckaye."

The only sounds in the vault are the rustling of manuscripts, the scuff of pencil on paper, and the singsong recitation of manuscript titles. The saintly names subdue our fears and cool our blood. They take us back four hundred years to the golden age of Timbuktu, an age of noblemen, holy men, and scholars. They restore our hearts to peace.

Hours later, in the middle of trunk sixty-five, the sunset prayer call jolts us out of our trance and reminds us of the world of men above.

My father yawns and stretches. "We are going to need more trunks," he says. "After sunset prayers, I will order twenty more from the blacksmith." He takes out his phone and moves toward the steps.

"Baba, wait," I say. "How are the rebels treating people in Gao and Kidal?"

"Don't worry so much." He turns to look at me. "The rebels' quarrel is with the government and the Malian army, not with simple people like us."

"What about the women?" I ask. "Are they—are they threatened?"

Baba starts plucking at his salt-and-pepper beard, and there are tears in his eyes. "I will keep you and your mother safe, my dear. Do you hear me? I swear I'll keep you safe."

He hesitates a moment, then reaches up and lifts his Kabyle musket off the wall.

"What are you doing, Baba? You always said that thing was just for decoration."

"It always was," he says.

☾

Manuscrits. Manuscripts. Dereeje. It doesn't matter what language—manuscripts are not sexy. Look at them lying there, thick wads of parchment covered in desert dust and Arabic scribble. Boring, right?

Wrong. Look closer. Take a manuscript from the shelf and set it down in the orange light of the paraffin lamp. As soon as you start to decipher the Arabic script, the words will reach up from the paper and grab you by the throat. You will start to tremble or dance or weep or jump for joy or gnash your teeth or groan or ululate or pray, and from that moment on, you will keep coming back to the manuscripts every day of your life.

What is written in these precious books?

Ha.

Astronomy so powerful it will bend your mind and give you vertigo. History so vivid you can taste the blood in your mouth. Love poems so passionate that your heart will beat out of your chest. God-talk so wild it will light up your face like the archangel Jibreel himself.

Magic too. Be careful, now. Imam Wangari says that a single word from the wrong manuscript will summon a djinni strong enough to pick you up, throw you across the room, and slam you into the wall so hard that every bone in your spine will shatter like a clay bead.

They are worth protecting, these manuscripts. That's why the owners of private manuscript collections are called *timbakewen*, Guardians. When the firstborn son of a Guardian turns seventeen, he swears a solemn oath and becomes a Guardian himself. If there is no son, a daughter may take the oath. Which is good news for me, of course.

My seventeenth birthday is still two years away, but I think about it all the time. I cannot wait to take the oath and become a Guardian. Just think of it: two thousand manuscripts in my care! I will cherish every single one.

> *Local wisdom of Timbuktu #1: Learn to ride fast, shoot high, and swim deep. But above all, learn to read wide.*

ᶜ

Timbuktu is dark tonight. The electricity has not yet come back on.

Baba drives a wooden pole into the middle of our courtyard and uses twists of wire to attach a battery-powered fluorescent light. The makeshift lamppost casts a circle of harsh white light, in which we arrange a dozen chairs and three large mats.

As the head of one of Timbuktu's oldest families, Baba has been an elder for as long as I can remember, and tonight he is hosting an emergency elders meeting. The elders used to meet at the town hall in Independence Square, but the threat of invasion has made the mayor nervous. He wants to have the meeting as close as possible to the military camp. He thinks it's safer here.

First to arrive is Baba's brother Uncle Abdel, who lives next door to us. He is Chief Librarian at the Ahmad Baba Library, and we see him every day. The other elders arrive on motorbikes: twelve heads of families, three imams, and some officials from the mayor's office. The place of honor, a comfortable basket chair, goes to the mayor himself. Like Sundiata, Lion King of Mali, he sits imperious in gold-embroidered robes.

The only person I don't recognize is the thin one with his shirt tucked into his trousers. I hear Baba introduce him to the others as Albert Sanon, the new headmaster of the school. Newly arrived from Bamako, poor man.

I squat on a small stool by the kitchen door, using the light in the courtyard to pick weevils out of a bucket of millet flour. No one pays me any attention, apart from Uncle Abdel, who raises his eyebrows in greeting.

Imam Cissé raps the ground three times with his ebony walking stick to bring the meeting to order. "News from the nomads," he says. "Redbeard's battalion has taken up their position in the desert to the north of the city. A Tuareg battalion is riding to meet them."

The mayor puffs out his cheeks. "Has the army been informed?" he asks.

"Of course."

"And the men are ready?"

The imam hesitates. "They are hunkered down inside the fort," he says. 'They won't admit it, but they are terrified of Redbeard. And they haven't been paid these last three months."

A long silence follows. We're done for. Our army garrison is hiding in their camp, and Timbuktu is open for the taking. It looks like Baba was wrong again.

Monsieur Sanon, the new headmaster, clears his throat. "Forgive me," he says. "Who is this Redbeard person?"

"A preacher," says the mayor. "The sort of preacher who shakes his fist a lot."

"His real name is Ould Hamaha," adds Imam Cissé. "Studied the Qur'an right here in Timbuktu and then in Mauritania. When he returned from Mauritania, he visited me at my mosque and asked me to grant him a preaching license for Timbuktu. At first I was impressed with him. He was a handsome young man and fiercely intelligent. He talked very elegantly about purity and law. But then he began to talk about killing."

"Killing infidels?"

"Not just infidels. Muslims. He told me that anyone who

commits adultery should be put to death, as should anyone who abandons the five daily prayers. I said to him at the time: "If your ideas catch on, Ould, we'll have to exterminate a third of the population of Timbuktu."

"What did he say to that?"

"'Kill a third to reform two thirds.' Those were his exact words. I thought he was joking until I looked at his face. And then I told him straight: 'Ould Hamaha, you will never preach at any of the mosques in Timbuktu, as long as I remain imam.'"

"Was that the last you saw of him?"

"For many years, yes. Rumor had it that he was traveling in Pakistan and Algeria, undergoing military training in special camps, and making contact with Salafist preachers and jihadists. In Mauritania the mujahidin called him Akka, like the letters *AK* in French."

"Automat Kalashnikov," explains Baba, noticing the school teacher's blank stare. "It's an assault rifle, favorite weapon of jihadists all over the world."

"I see."

"By the time Redbeard came back to Mali, he was angrier and more dangerous than ever. Well funded too. He founded a battalion called the Defenders of Faith, and he started touring the villages of the north, preaching and recruiting. He knows our young men are bored, so he offers them excitement and adventure. He knows they are confused, so he gives them meaning and purpose. He knows they are angry, so he gives them an enemy to hate. And he also gives their parents cold, hard cash. Young men are flocking to join his battalion and we can't do a thing about it."

We can't do a thing about it. Just my luck to be born in Timbuktu, a city of malnourished soldiers and toothless old men.

What chance do they have against the youth and passion of the mujahidin? None at all.

I pick another weevil out of the millet flour and squeeze it between finger and thumb until I hear it pop.

☾

An hour later the food is ready.

There are four serving bowls: one for the steaming slabs of millet, one for the baobab-leaf sauce, one for drinking water, and one for hand-washing water.

"We'll carry two each," Mama tells me. "Do your humblest walk, and make sure you curtsy when you set the bowls down."

We take the bowls out, place them on the ground in the middle of the circle, and retreat to the kitchen.

Mama shines her flashlight in my face. "What was that?" she says.

"That was my humble walk."

"You looked like a constipated duck."

"Sorry, Mama. I don't really have a humble walk."

"You don't have a humble anything, Kadija." She scrapes some leftover millet and sauce into a bowl, and we squat to eat. "Don't look so glum," she says. "Timbuktu is not going to be attacked."

"How do you know?"

"It's obvious," she says. "Now that the rebels have Kidal and Gao, they won't want to spread themselves too thin. Besides, they would be insane to attack such a famous city. Everybody in the world has heard of Timbuktu."

"Yes, but most people think it's—" I break off, not wanting to upset her.

"Most people think it's what?"

"They think it's an imaginary place."

23

There. I've said it.

Mama's hand stops abruptly on its way to her mouth. "Don't talk nonsense, Kadija. Timbuktu is the best-known city in Africa."

"It isn't, Mama. Aisha looked up Timbuktu in her English dictionary, and it just said, 'Any far-off place.'"

Mama's eyes widen. For a moment I think she is going to cry, but instead her face goes hard and proud. "Aisha Diabaté is an ignorant girl. It's no surprise to me that her book is ignorant as well."

She clicks her tongue in her cheek to signal the end of the conversation.

"If Timbuktu does fall," I persist, "do you think we—"

"Timbuktu will *not* fall," snaps Mama, "but I'll tell you what will happen. All this fear and confusion will drive the price of food sky high. Tomorrow you and I will pay a visit to the tomb of Sidi Ahmed ben Amar. We will dance there and pray for God's provision."

"Or we could just buy a sack of millet before the price goes up," I say.

"Don't be impertinent," she snaps.

I'm not trying to be impertinent. And I don't even mind visiting the tombs of the saints. I just don't like going with Mama. To see her dance, you would think she was being attacked by bees.

Wisdom of Timbuktu #2 : To receive the blessings of the saints, visit the tombs of the saints. Shrine time is never wasted.

When the elders have left, we go to the Sidi Yahya Mosque in Independence Square for night prayers. Mama and I usually do night prayers at home, but tonight is different. There is special power in communal prayer, Baba says.

Other people's fathers must have said the same thing because Independence Square is full of families—a million moonlit worshippers flip-flopping toward the mosque.

As we enter the Sidi Yahya compound, Mama nudges me and points to a closed door on the left side of the mosque. It is an ancient Timbuktu door, like the door of our manuscript vault, but its silver rivets are shaped like crescents and stars. The Door of Heaven, we call it.

Back in the days when tourists still came to Timbuktu, the Door of Heaven was a big attraction. I used to watch them as they stood in front of it with their rucksacks and their sunburned noses, chortling stupidly, and daring each other to open it. But that's the thing. No one can open the Door of Heaven, however hard they try. There is not even a handle. Imam Cissé says that the Door of Heaven will stay firmly closed until the return of the Prophet Isa and the end of time itself.

"See that, Kadi?" Mama whispers, looping an arm round my waist. "It's not the end of the world. Not just yet."

I kick off my sandals outside the mosque and take my place with the other women at the back of the congregation. *"Allahu Akbar!"* groans Imam Cissé in the front row, and the ritual begins.

We stand.

We bow.

We lean forward until the crisscross weave of the prayer mat prints itself on our foreheads.

It's hot inside the mosque. The sun set two hours ago, but the heat of the day still radiates from the mud-brick walls and columns. As I straighten up from my first prostration, a bead of perspiration forms on the nape of my neck and trickles slowly down my back.

In the row in front of me, a little girl is praying. She has a special prayer cushion inscribed with the seven sacred verses of Al-Fatiha, but she is having trouble reading from it and kneeling on it at the same time. Back and forth she bobs and squirms, and her prayers are interspersed with little whimpers of frustration.

After the last prayer cycle, we kneel with our hands on our thighs and recite the Tashahhud. "Peace be upon us," we say, "and upon those who are righteous servants of Allah." I screw my eyes tight shut and press my fingernails into the palm of my hand. "Peace be upon us," I mutter under my breath. "Please, Lord." By the end of prayer time, I am truly praying.

Prayer is like that. When you start off, you hear only your own heartbeat. By the end, you hear only His.

At the end of the service, Imam Cissé hobbles to the front with his prayer beads and his ebony walking stick. When he picks up the microphone, a blast of feedback screams from the amp behind him. There are yelps of alarm all over the mosque. We are on edge and we know it.

The old imam frowns and steps away from the amp.

"Timbuktu has been invaded before," he says. "In the course of history, our great city has been invaded six times. It was invaded by the sultan of Mossi, by Sunni Ali, by Pasha Zarqun, by Askia Muhammad, by Sultan Al-Mansur of Marrakech, and by Marshal Joffre. Each time, Timbuktu survived. You know as well as I do that the soul of Timbuktu is not in its city walls, its buildings, or its institutions. The soul of Timbuktu is in the writings of its scholars, the tombs of its saints, and the worship of its God. People come and people go, but the soul of Timbuktu remains untouched. Remember God, my sons and daughters, and do not let worry gain a foothold. Sleep well and rise for morning prayers with a smile on your lips, whatever the day might bring."

People come and people go.

Imam Cissé means well, of course. He is trying to encourage us. He is trying to help us see things in perspective. But when I leave the mosque, my knees are shaking, and I can't for the life of me remember which step I left my sandals on.

☾

In the month of April it is too hot to sleep in the bedroom, or anywhere inside the house. My parents sleep in the open air in the middle of the courtyard and I sleep on the flat earthen roof of the house. A tree trunk leaning at forty-five degrees leads from the courtyard up to the roof, with twelve deep notches for steps.

I fetch a light cotton wraparound from my bedroom and half fill a bucket from the water barrel in the kitchen. I balance the bucket on my head, say good night to Mama and Baba, and scoot up the tree-trunk staircase two notches at a time.

"I don't like Kadi sleeping up there on her own," I hear Mama say. "Maybe she should sleep in the vault tonight."

"With only one exit and a wall of hay in front of the door? No, my dear, that roof is the safest place in the house. If any fighting breaks out, we'll go running up there to join her, just you wait!"

Their voices fade away as I carry my bucket to the far side of the roof and set it down. Squatting naked under the stars, I use a gourd to tip cool water over my head and back.

I can't help glancing down into the compound next door, where dark figures crouch round a bowl of food: Uncle Abdel, Aunt Juma, dear cousin Kamisa. Yusuf too. I recognize the sleek curves of his ngoni, still slung across his back.

I wring the water from my hair, dip my cotton wraparound in what remains of the water, and go to my millet-stalk mat.

Wisdom of Timbuktu #3: Go to bed with a wet cotton sheet across your body, and rewet it throughout the night. It's the only way you will get any sleep.

Some nights I make up songs. With the stars so near, the words and music come easily.

Some nights I smuggle a manuscript to bed and pore over it by the light of a paraffin lamp.

Some nights I talk to Aisha on the phone, and we whoop and gossip at three francs a minute until our credit runs out.

I decide to ring Aisha, but neither of us is in the mood for whooping. She is worried about her cousins in Gao. She has been trying to ring them, but the phone network there is down.

"Don't worry," I tell her. "Baba says the rebels won't harm civilians. The only people in danger are Malian soldiers."

"OK."

There is a long silence. In the stars above me, Ali the warrior brandishes his sword and shield.

"My mother is cross with you," I say, "because your dictionary thinks Timbuktu is 'any far-off place.'"

Aisha sighs. "Right now I wish it *wasn't* a real place. No rebels, no fear, no stress, just a beautiful mythical city in the middle of the desert."

"A city paved with gold?"

"Solid gold. And me, a beautiful mythical Timbuktu princess with tortoiseshell hair extensions and a mysterious tattoo on my shoulder. And you, one of my mythical serving maids, almost beautiful, but not quite."

"Almost beautiful, but not quite!" I burst out laughing. "In that case I shall be almost loyal, but not quite. I shall run away in the middle of the night with all your mythical jewels."

Aisha hoots. "See if I care! You can't sell mythical jewels, girl, and you can't wear them either."

"Kadi!" My father's voice rises from the courtyard below. "Who's up there with you?"

"Baba, please, I'm on the phone!" I shout.

Two rapid beeps and Aisha is gone. My credit has run out and I am alone beneath the stars.

☾

Midnight, and I still can't sleep. I sit on the balustrade at the edge of the roof and gaze out over the roofs of Timbuktu.

Down below me is Askia, a wide street named after one of Mali's greatest warriors. It is the oldest street in Timbuktu, with the vast mud-brick ramparts of the Djinguereber Mosque at its northern end and the whitewashed buildings of Independence Square to the south. This time last week, the street glowed with the embers of a hundred charcoal stoves—huddles of men and women drinking sweet tea and telling improbable stories. To-night there is no glow. The people of Timbuktu are all at home, a-praying in their beds.

The Sidi el Beckaye Fort is set well back from the road on the edge of the city. Its walls loom high and impenetrable. Out of the corner of my eye, I sense a flicker of movement against the wall.

I shut my eyes for a few seconds to adjust them to darkness. When I open them again, the shape is still there. It is a man, or maybe a boy, dressed all in black, with a small rucksack high on his shoulders. He scurries along the base of the high wall, moving quickly and quietly on the balls of his feet.

As I watch, the boy crouches down and reaches into his backpack. He straightens up quickly and wheels his arms as if flinging something high into the air.

A slither and a quiet clink, and I realize what is happening. I tie my wrap across my body and run to tell my parents.

"Wake up," I hiss. "There's someone outside the military camp. He threw some sort of hook. I think he's going to climb the wall."

"I'm coming." Baba's voice rises from the darkness. "I'll be right there."

By the time I get back to the edge of the roof, the shadow is already halfway up the wall and climbing fast.

This is not how I thought it would start. I had expected to see flashes of mortar fire on a distant horizon. Not this black-clad boy dangling on a rope before my nose.

"Where is he?" Baba arrives on my right, his voice tense with adrenaline. "Can you still see him?"

"Right there. Near the top of the wall."

Mama is running across the roof, arms stretched wide like she's trying to catch a chicken. "Don't fire!" she cries. "You're going to get us killed!"

Too late, out of the corner of my eye, I catch a glimpse of ivory and silver. Baba is aiming his musket. A bright light and a bang. A gust of hot gunpowder billows out of the chamber.

The force of the recoil makes Baba stagger backward.

"I think I hit him!" he cries.

The right side of my face and neck feel like a colony of fire ants is stinging them. I run to the water bucket and scoop handfuls of water over my cheek.

Shouts of alarm and barked commands sound from the military camp below.

Baba is rejoicing. "I got him!" he cries. "He's lying in the road. *Astaghfirullah!* God forgive me."

Mama is gaping and wittering at my side. "Let me look at you, Kadi," cries Mama, shining a flashlight in my eyes. "Hold still and let me look at you."

"Turn that light off!" hisses Baba.

"Aloe vera sap," says Mama. 'That's what you need."

"I said, turn that light off!"

A deafening *crack*, and Mama throws herself on top of me.

"What was that?" My voice is muffled by Mama's jasmine-scented cleavage.

Another bullet hisses overhead.

"Get off the roof!" urges Baba.

We wriggle across the roof, all elbows and bottoms, and slither down the tree-trunk ladder. As I reach the ground, a wave of sudden pressure knocks me sideways. An explosion, not in our courtyard, but very close.

"Everyone down to the vault!" shouts Baba.

Mama crouches in the corner of the compound. "I'm picking aloe vera!" she shouts.

She waddles back to us with a handful of fat, serrated leaves and shines her flashlight into Marimba's enclosure. He is dashing round like a dust devil, with frightened eyes and pricked-back ears.

"No way," I say. "I'm not going in there."

Baba vaults the gate. He grabs Marimba round the neck and tries to hold him still.

"Go," Mama tells me. "Go now."

I sprint round the edge of the enclosure and dive behind the hay bales. Mama follows. Baba unlocks the secret door and chivies us down the stairs.

"Only one exit, with a wall of hay in front of it," mutters Mama. "Isn't that what you said?"

"Yes," snaps Baba, "but less risky than jumping around on the roof, don't you think?"

"Who was jumping around?" cries Mama. "I wasn't jumping around."

"We could hardly stay hidden with you shouting and waving your flashlight about."

"Stay hidden? You fired a musket, you old goat!"

Down in the vault Mama breaks the fleshy, aloe vera leaves and squeezes the transparent slime into the hollow of her hand.

"Hold still," she says, rubbing the cool sap onto my face and neck. "God be praised, it's just a surface burn."

A massive explosion sounds above us and a smattering of earth falls on my head from the roof of the vault.

"It's not going to cave in, is it, Baba?"

"Impossible," says Baba, "*inshallah*."

"It won't cave in," says Mama, firmly. "Remember God, and do not let worry gain a foothold. That's what Imam Cissé told us."

"Your mother's right," says Baba. "We should do *dhikr*."

He tightens the wick of the paraffin lamp so that the flame shrinks to a frail, orange glow. We sit down on the cool earth floor and hold hands.

"*Hasbi rabijal Allah*," says Baba. "Our defense is in God."

"*Hasbi rabijal Allah*," we repeat. "*Hasbi rabijal Allah. Hasbi rabijal Allah . . .*"

My racing heart begins to slow. At first I am aware of the Arabic syllables and the light touch of my parents' hands, but soon my tongue takes over and I speak the words without thinking about them. Before long I forget my parents, and then I forget myself.

Our defense is in God. In my mind's eye I see Timbuktu cocooned within a bead of amber. Our defense is in God.

Wisdom of Timbuktu #4: At the beginning of a session, you do dhikr. *By the end,* dhikr *does you.*

Manuscript 11,045: the tarikh of Sidi Yahya

One Friday night in the year 1440, the imam of the Sankore Mosque had a dream. He dreamed that the Prophet, peace be upon him, was telling him to build a third mosque in Timbuktu. He shared his dream with the city elders, and they decided to build a new mosque between the Djinguereber Mosque and the Sankore Mosque.

"Where will we find an imam for the new mosque?" people asked.

"God will provide an imam," the elders replied.

The front door of the mosque remained locked for several years, and then one evening a holy man arrived from Oualata in Mauritania. He was dressed all in white and was followed by three camels and a well-washed band of students.

"Where are the keys to this mosque?" he asked.

Recognizing the man as God's intended imam for the new mosque, the neighbors of the mosque gave him the keys.

The man was Sidi Yahya.

Sidi Yahya lived a simple life in Timbuktu. He had no riches, animals, or commerce. Whenever he received a gift, whether sugar, cotton, or gold, he gave it immediately to the poor.

One day an old woman came to see Sidi Yahya. "Man of God and sheikh of sheikhs," she said, "have pity on a poor servant of God who has lost all hope."

Sidi Yahya was moved by the woman's tears and he prayed to God on her behalf. When at last he opened his eyes he saw a company of djinn passing in front of his gate on their way to a djinni wedding.

"Dear woman," he said, "I want you to imagine you are at a wedding ceremony. Open your mouth and let your tongue trill to high heaven."

The woman could not see the djinn, but she did what the saint commanded. Although she was feeling sad and hopeless, she raised her head, closed her eyes, and began to ululate.

"Yu-yu-yu-yu-yu!" trilled the old woman, and the populace of Timbuktu wondered at the sound.

All of a sudden a whirlwind of dust began to gyrate in the air. Out of the center of the wind flew a purple velvet pouch, landing with a thud in the old woman's lap. She opened her eyes, undid the drawstrings of the pouch, and stared, for the pouch was brimming with grains of purest gold.

May the blessings of Sidi Yahya be upon us all.

Ali

When at last I open my eyes, I see my namesake in the stars above me, wielding the good sword Zulfiqaar. The three bright stars of Ali's belt shine down on me and bring me peace. Ali the warrior, Lion of God, protector of Muhammad at the Battle of Uhud, commander at the Battle of Khaybar, glorious hero of the Battle of Hunayn. *King of the Brave, Lion of God with the strength of God.*

Bursts of gunfire sputter near and far, with an occasional chest-filling boom from a grenade.

The battle! The mission! It's still going on!

I jump to my feet—and collapse in pain.

"Don't try to stand," says a voice by my side. Omar is sitting cross-legged next to me, cradling an AK-47 in his lap.

"Where am I?"

"You are in the military camp. You hurt your ankle when you fell, and you hit your head as well. Your battle is over, Ali."

"Where are the others?"

"Out," says Omar. "They are helping Litni and his men to secure the airport and the radio station. They told me to stay here and look after you."

"What about Redbeard? Is he here yet?"

"Not yet."

I sit up and rub my left ankle. "I fell, you say?"

"Like Lucifer from heaven!"

I should be out there, fighting shoulder to shoulder with my brothers. Instead, I am sitting here rubbing my useless ankle. I have imagined this battle a hundred times, but never once did I see it like this.

"The hard work is done," says Omar. "Praise be to God, the city has fallen."

There is no joy in his voice, only tiredness.

"My namesake Ali slew twenty-seven men at the Battle of Badr," I say. "And I slew none at all."

"It does not matter," whispers Omar. "You threw the metal claw perfectly, just like in training. You gave us our way in."

"There are a thousand shepherds in Goundam who could have thrown the claw."

"Maybe, maybe not," says Omar. "Do you know what Chief Litni's men are calling you?"

"Idiot?"

"No. They're calling you Lee."

"So they should. It's my warrior name."

"Not Ali, but Lee, as in Bruce Lee, the ninja in those movies we used to watch. They are calling us the Ninjas and they are calling you Lee."

My heart fills up with pride, but I must not let it show. "I'm nothing like Bruce Lee," I mutter. "Bruce Lee would never have fallen off that rope."

"If he got shot, he would."

Omar holds the backlight of his phone to my goatskin satchel and shows me a small, round hole in the leather. Then he reaches into the satchel and pulls out my grenade.

The grenade rattles when he shakes it.

"There's something trapped inside," I say.

"Correct, my friend. Your grenade stopped a musket ball!"

I grab his phone and shine the light on a tiny hole in the grenade casing.

"It's a miracle," I gasp. "Why didn't the musket ball set the grenade off?"

"Once the casing of a grenade gets punctured, it can't explode, not even if you pull the pin."

"*Allahu Akbar.*"

"You should keep it as a souvenir," says Omar. "God loves you, Ali Konana."

Still clutching the miracle grenade, I lie down and close my eyes. My head and my ankle are throbbing. Tiredness spreads warmly through my body, mingling with the pain.

"Don't tell anyone about the grenade," I hear myself murmur as I fall asleep. "Let it be a secret between ourselves and God."

"OK."

"And Omar—tell them to stop calling me Lee. Movies are *haram.*"

☾

When I wake again, prayer calls are blaring from nearby mosques. As soon as I make out the cadences of one call, another overtakes it, like shepherds singing a round. They have guts, these prayer callers. In any other city, the callers would lock themselves in their houses during a battle, and the townspeople would miss all five of their appointments with God.

I open my eyes and see the scorpion directly above me. The scorpion constellation is always chasing Ali the warrior across the sky, but it never catches him. When the scorpion rises in the east, Ali sets in the west, and so it will be for all eternity. Ali is blessed. He always gets away.

I see the grenade in my right hand and remember what Omar said about my near escape from death. I rub my thumb over the tortoiseshell grooves. *God loves you, Ali Konana.*

"Good morning," says Omar.

"Morning," I say. "Is Redbeard here yet?"

"No, not yet."

The sky is beginning to lighten in the east, and I can make out the shapes of men moving round the camp. Charcoal stoves glow in the lingering dark, and the bitter smell of Tuareg tea hangs in the air. Chief Litni's men brought their teapots and stoves in their kit bags alongside their grenades and ammunition. Tea addicts, every one of them.

Omar is sitting with his back pressed against a squat, mud-brick pyramid.

"Is that Tamba-Tamba's shrine?" I ask.

"That's right," says Omar. "His bones protect the garrison from attack. They seem to have failed this time."

Omar brings a bowl of water for morning prayer. I wash my hands three times, and then my mouth, nose, ears, and feet. When Omar washes his hands, I can't help noticing the blood under his nails.

"Yours?" I ask.

"Hilal's." Omar takes a deep breath. "We buried him just before sunrise."

"God!" I cry.

The word comes from deep within me, a long drawn-out

39

groan of grief and prayer. Hilal, the jester, is dead. We will never laugh again.

"*Paradise has been decorated for him,*" quotes Omar softly, "*and beautiful women are calling upon him—'Come, oh commander with the order of God'—and they are dressed in their best attire.*"

"Where is Hamza?"

"He has gone back to his village, to give his parents the news."

Omar's voice is close to breaking, and mine as well. If we talk any more, we will cry, and that would shame us both. So instead we pray. I lean on him to recite Al-Fatiha, and then we kneel to pray.

I think of Hilal's brother trudging across the dunes toward Lake Télé, his feet entrenched in sand, his heart in grief.

At breakfast time, Redbeard is still not here. Omar and I eat dates and peanuts, while ragged vultures gaze down on us from the top of the wall.

Omar tells me more about the battle. He tells me I was shot by a sniper on a nearby roof, but he can't remember which one.

"Hamza dragged you to safety," he says, "and the rest of us went over the wall, just like we planned. Hilal was first, but he spent too long rigging the rappel rope. A sentry saw him."

"The sentry shot Hilal?"

"Yes." Omar winces at the memory. "And I shot the sentry."

"*You* shot the sentry?"

"I got lucky," he says and shrugs. "After that, it was easy. We split into two groups, like Redbeard taught us. Four of us laid down covering fire and the other four rappelled down the rope and fought through to the gates."

"*Allahu Akbar,*" I murmur. "God is great."

"Once we got to the gates and opened them for Litni and his men, the infidels had no chance. Eight got shot in the battle, and the rest of them surrendered."

"What happened to the ones who surrendered?"

Omar takes a date stone out of his mouth and throws it across the compound. "The Tuaregs shot them."

I stare at him. "You're not serious?"

"You know what Tuaregs are like."

I close my eyes and stick my fingers in my ears. I don't want to hear any more. Executing prisoners of war was never part of our training. The thought of it makes me feel sick.

When I open my eyes at last, Omar is still munching dates.

"They can't do that," I say weakly. "It's against God's law."

"Maybe, maybe not," he says, pushing his glasses up his nose. "There are two schools of thought."

With Omar there are always two schools of thought. He probably thinks there are two schools of thought about whether sand is sandy.

☪

The Ninjas return jubilant. They have helped the Tuaregs to secure the airport and the radio station, and now they have a few hours to eat, sleep, and swap battle stories. They have brought me bandages and painkillers from a nearby pharmacy.

"Thanks," I say. "I did not think the pharmacies would be open for business this morning."

"The Tuaregs have opened everything for business," says Jabir, laughing. "They are roaming around town taking whatever they want. Food. Cars. Sheep. It's crazy out there."

"Looting!" I drop the pharmacy bag in the dust. "It's common theft."

"Actually," says Omar, "it could be interpreted as *ghazwa*, raiding, which would be—"

"Shut up, Omar," I say, reaching into my satchel for my phone. "I'm calling Redbeard."

41

I try several times before getting through, but at last Red-beard answers. He is pleased that we have taken Timbuktu, but he is angry about the executions and the looting.

"We work with Chief Litni because he is useful," he says, "but his soldiers are not fit to call themselves Muslims. A thug who prays five times a day is still a thug."

"What do you want us to do?"

"Do nothing," says Redbeard. "We will be with you in three days. Keep yourselves pure and wait for—"

The line goes dead. I have run out of credit.

"Three days!" I cry. "Redbeard is planning to come in *three days*. That wasn't the plan. What is he doing in the desert that needs three days?"

"It's simple," says Jabir. "He wants life in Timbuktu to get worse before it gets better. When he carries the black standard into town three days from now, the people of Timbuktu will welcome him like a savior. He's a clever old fox is Redbeard."

"He's not an old fox," I snap. "He's our master. Show some respect."

Jabir glances at my ankles, and I can tell what he's thinking: What did you do in the Battle of Timbuktu, Ali? Did you sleep well?

I lie down and close my eyes. My ankle is throbbing, and my head as well.

Maybe I will take those painkillers after all. When my ankle is better, I will go to the pharmacy and pay in full.

Later that morning we go on patrol in three Save the Chil-dren pickup trucks. Litni and his men take the comfortable seats inside the trucks, and we have to ride in a trailer. Omar and the others lift me into the trailer and then hop in themselves. It's a squash, and the metal underneath us is already hot from the sun.

The trucks drive out of the gates of the military camp and into the dusty streets of Timbuktu.

I already know this city a little bit. My parents used to bring me here on the feast days of Tabaski and Mouloud, to pray and celebrate with the multitudes. On those special days, everyone was dressed to impress in their pristine feast-day robes. There were women crouching at the side of the road making pancakes, young men selling mobile phone cases and cassettes, old men grasping each other's hands and elbows in respectful greeting.

Back in those days, there were tourists too—men and women with lopsided turbans and sunburned noses. The men wore T-shirts and shorts like little boys, and the women had bare shoulders. The people of Timbuktu seemed to love the tourists, even though they talked loudly, took photos without asking, and had no fear of God in them at all. With my own eyes, I saw a white man saunter into the Sidi Yahya Mosque without even taking his sandals off. But when Muhammad Zaarib and his gang started kidnapping tourists and holding them for ransom, the tourists stopped coming to Timbuktu, God be praised.

Today the streets of the city are deserted. Sometimes I catch a pair of eyes peering from a crack in a door or between shuttered windows—dark, fearful eyes which appear for a moment and then disappear again.

We drive through Independence Square and past the square turrets of the Sidi Yahya Mosque. The Grand Market is still and silent, and many of the shop fronts have been vandalized. Corrugated metal panels have been torn to shreds by pickaxes, and the empty shelves bear witness to a morning of frenzied looting. Rice, palm oil, tea, sugar, dates, biscuits—the Tuaregs have taken everything. Even the charcoal market has been plundered for the sake of morning tea.

I used to love coming to Timbuktu, even if it was only once or twice a year. There were foosball tables on every corner. There were televisions showing distant soccer matches. There were pretty girls with tattooed lips and earrings the size of oranges. Best of all, on the corner of the Grand Market, there was a fiery cabinet of whole, roasting chickens, which sizzled and crackled as they rotated on their skewers. I bought one once, and squatted out of sight behind a donkey cart and ate the whole thing there and then. Paradise.

I was wrong to think that Timbuktu was paradise. I can see clearly now, thanks to Redbeard, and I know what a dustbowl of godlessness the city is.

We drive around the Well of Old Buktu, back through Independence Square, and then up Askia. Like everywhere else, the street is deserted.

As we pass under the shadow of the Djinguereber Mosque, I close my eyes and wince.

"Ankle?" asks Omar.

"No," I tell him. "Memories."

☾

Two years ago my parents took my sister and me to Timbuktu on the feast day of Mouloud, the birthday of the Prophet. The crowds in the streets around the Djinguereber Mosque were massive. Too many people in too small a space, squeezed together like goats in a market truck, and the pressure increasing all the time. None of us saw the danger until it was upon us. One moment we were rubbing shoulders and singing, then suddenly we were jostling and shouting and fighting for breath. "Don't let yourself go under!" That's what my mother kept screaming. "Don't let yourself go under!"

I grabbed my sister under her arms and hoisted her up until

she was half above the crowd. Someone else got hold of her foot and pushed her clear. "Head for the wall, Safi!" I shouted, and off she went, too dazed to cry, clambering over people's shawls and turbans to safety.

The boy next me, a young Qur'anic student, was not so lucky. With his blue lips and dilated pupils he looked more djinni than human. He was staring straight at me, and his blue lips kept mouthing the same thing over and over: *Wallam, wallam, wallam.* Help me. But by now my arms were pinned to my sides and there was nothing I could do. The poor boy choked to death under an infinite, blue sky—he and twenty-five others.

After the Djinguereber Crush, our family never came to Timbuktu again. We stayed home in Goundam, even on feast days, and prayed with our neighbors in the tumbledown mosque on the shore of the lake.

☾

Our three patrol trucks arrive at the top of Askia, where the street widens out into a public square. On the north side of the square, with the sun shining fiercely on its whitewashed facade, stands the Ahmad Baba Library. A human chain surrounds the library. Young and old, women and men, the citizens of Timbuktu hold hands in the sweltering sun.

"So this is where everyone is," says Jabir, grinning his buck-toothed grin.

"That's Timbuktu for you," says Omar. "They don't protect their homes or shops or banks. They protect their manuscripts!"

"Hardly protecting," scoffs Jabir. "It's not like they're armed, is it?"

The three patrol trucks drive up to the front of the library and Chief Litni winds down the window. "Who is in charge?" he barks.

A tall, thin man steps forward out of line. Intelligent, black eyes shine out between the folds of his turban. "Peace be upon you," he says. "I am Abdel Diallo, Chief Librarian."

Chief Litni looks from the librarian to the pathetic human chain. "If hens guard the palace," he says, "the king will not sleep soundly."

The librarian forces a smile. "Perhaps you've never seen an angry hen."

Litni opens the door of the car and climbs out, his AK-47 dangling across his body. "Show me, then," he says. "What does an angry hen look like?"

Abdel Diallo looks down at the Tuareg's gun with big, watery eyes. He swallows hard. "What do you want, *monsieur*?"

"Manuscripts," says the Tuareg chief. "The manuscripts in this building are worth millions, are they not?"

"You have already looted our markets," says Abdel Diallo. "You must leave our manuscripts in peace."

"Must?" cries Chief Litni, looking round at his men. "Did the librarian just say *must* to *me*?"

The Tuaregs hop out of the trucks and gather, armed and grinning, behind their chief.

I reach across to Omar and snatch his phone from the top pocket of his shirt. My fingers fly across the keys.

Urgent. Litni looting manuscripts. Advise.

"Step aside, librarian," says Litni, and his right hand drifts down toward the stock of his AK-47. "I want those manuscripts."

Abdel Diallo steps back into line and grasps his neighbors' hands so that the human chain is once again complete. "The soul of Timbuktu is in the writings of its scholars," the librarian quotes softly, "and we will protect those writings to our dying breath."

"As you wish," Chief Litni says, and squeezes the trigger of his assault rifle.

CRACK!

The petrified protectors of the library jump and squeal as Litni's bullets fly over their heads and lodge in the whitewashed wall above the door.

"This is not right," I whisper to Omar. "We came to Timbuktu to teach the way of God, not to steal manuscripts."

Omar shrugs. He is terrified of this angry Tuareg. We all are.

Abdel Diallo clears his throat and starts to chant, pronouncing in a quavering voice the words of some ancient vow.

"I solemnly swear to guard the manuscripts of Timbuktu entrusted to my family by the saints of old. I will protect them in times of peace and in times of war, in times of planting and in times of harvesting, in times of joy and in times of sorrow. I will protect them from fire and from flood, from wizards and from thieves, from giants and from djinn. God grant me the wisdom of the horse, the stubbornness of the ox, and the cunning of the—"

"Shut up!"

Chief Litni strides forward, seizes the librarian by the scruff of his robe, tears him free of his neighbors' hands, and slams him with a hideous thud against the library door. Litni tries the door, but it's locked, and then presses the barrel of his assault rifle into the soft underside of the librarian's chin.

"Give me the key," he snarls.

"No," says Abdel Diallo.

"Then I shall take it from your corpse!" shouts Litni. In one swift movement he cycles the bolt of his AK-47 to remove the spent cartridge, and puts his finger back on the trigger.

TRILL, TRILL. TRILL, TRILL. Somewhere in the swaths of Chief Litni's off-white robes, a mobile phone is ringing.

He puts the phone to his ear and listens.

Am I imagining it, or have the Tuareg's shoulders slumped?

He replaces the phone and whispers something inaudible in the librarian's ear.

"What's going on?" mouths Omar.

"I don't know."

With a deep sigh, Abdel Diallo hands over a silvery key. The Tuareg turns, throws it to one of his men, and juts his chin toward a sleek Land Cruiser parked in the shade to the west of the library.

"Another patrol vehicle for Azawad!" shouts Litni, but the triumph in his voice is forced and his eyes are sparkling with rage.

"I thought he wanted the key to the library," whispers Omar.

"He did."

"Who were you texting just now?"

"Redbeard."

I glance at the men and women in the human chain, who no longer show any emotion. They stand impassive in the sun, holding hands, and gazing straight ahead.

☾

Two days later Redbeard arrives in Timbuktu with the rest of our battalion. They arrive in four white Land Cruisers overflowing with fighters and weapons. One of the fighters in the back of each vehicle is carrying the black standard, the glorious flag of jihad.

"They're here!" cries Omar, rushing out of the camp. We follow him into the street, grinning stupidly under our turbans. I still cannot walk on my own, but I have made myself a pair of wooden crutches to swing around on.

The sleek white trucks brake sharply, filling the air with choking dust. Redbeard leaps down and embraces us each in turn. "Ninjas of God, well done!" he cries. "I salute each one of you."

Chief Litni is the last to greet Redbeard. They do not embrace, and there is a cold reluctance in their handshake.

"Peace be with you, Chief Litni," says Redbeard. "Your men have been busy, I hear."

"The first days of an occupation are always difficult," replies the Tuareg chief. "There are eating and sleeping arrangements to be organized. Pockets of resistance to be smothered. Municipal authorities to be instructed. You are yawning, Redbeard. Are you tired?"

"Somewhat."

Litni's eyes darken, but he keeps his cool. "You should get some rest."

"Excellent idea," says Redbeard. "You take your men south, and set up camp at the airport. My battalion and I will sleep here in the barracks."

The Tuareg scowls. "The dust from your tires has not yet settled, Redbeard. Are you already giving me orders?"

"Yes," says Redbeard, and a wide-eyed smile lights up his grizzled face. "Now that we are in control of Timbuktu, I no longer have to pretend that you and I are equals."

☾

The sun is high in the sky, and the Defenders of Faith are preparing for a feast.

Plastic mats are beaten and unrolled. Bottles of warm Coca-Cola are uncapped and laid out in rows. Saharan salt and black pepper are pounded in a mortar. *POK-POK-POK*, this meal will be heavenly. We have three things to celebrate: our victory in the Battle of Timbuktu, the reunion of our battalion, and the departure of Chief Litni's thugs. They are setting up camp at the airport, just like Redbeard told them to.

A fire is burning by the north wall of the compound. Three

cauldrons of rice and onions perch on the outer coals, while in the center two headless goats revolve on a spit. Omar and I crouch on our haunches nearby, basking in the smell of cooking meat and listening to droplets of goat fat hissing on the coals. A happy day indeed.

I bend down and write the date in the sand with my finger. "April 2, 2012."

At two o'clock the goats are still not cooked, so we pray on an empty stomach, kneeling and bowing in front of our untouched Coca-Cola. Then we sit on our mats and raise our palms to heaven in grateful supplication.

"You must be vigilant, boys," says Redbeard, when we have finished praying. "Put a man in the desert with only his Book and his gun, and he will easily master himself. But make that man a ruler of one of the greatest cities on earth and his worldly self will rise again. In the coming days and weeks, you will be tempted in every way, but you must not give in. This is Timbuktu and you are *Ansar Dine*, Defenders of Faith."

"Defenders of Faith," I write in the sand, underlining it with a long squiggle.

"The goat is cooked," says Redbeard. "Let the feast begin, before the Coca-Cola gets flat."

We gorge ourselves on the flavored rice and then start on the meat. As we eat, Redbeard tells us how he called Chief Litni at just the right moment and ordered him not to loot the manuscripts.

"I told him straight," says Redbeard. "'Litni,'" I said, "'if you lay a hand on a single one of those manuscripts, I will tie the end of your turban to the back leg of your camel and fire off thirty rounds right by its ear.'"

We laugh like hyenas and slap each other on the back. I'm

sure he did not say that to Litni, but it's a good story, which is the important thing.

"I'm going to die of pleasure," groans Omar, snapping a bone and sucking out the marrow. "Even at the feast of Ibrahim I never get this much meat."

As always, we cast lots for the goats' heads, which have been roasted whole.

Muhammad Zaarib draws a winning lot. Zaarib is one of the few grown men in our battalion. In a former life, he was a blacksmith with arms like iron bands. He has waged holy war all over West Africa and knows more about jihad and sharia than the rest of us put together.

Zaarib takes the head and raises it triumphantly in the air. "God is great!" he cries. "I haven't held a head since that incident with the French spy in the Ifoghas mountains."

The other boys howl with laughter. They're in that sort of mood. They'd laugh at anything.

Zaarib chews the goat's eyes with an open mouth, then turns the skull over to dig out the brain and tongue.

I feel sick. The killing of the French spy was before our time, but we've all heard the story, and some of the boys even have the video on their phone. I'm not saying Zaarib was wrong to kill the hostage, just that he took too much pleasure in it.

"Peace be upon you all."

Hamza is back. With glassy eyes, he surveys the rows of merrymakers and the piles of discarded goat bones.

"And on you," we intone.

Redbeard jumps up and embraces Hamza. "Do not grieve, boy," he says. "Your brother died in the cause of God. His sins are forgiven."

Hamza nods like an agama lizard, but his eyes are dull.

"A martyr feels no pain in death," says Redbeard, "except a brief pang like the sting of a bee. Your brother is alive in Paradise and praying for seventy of his relatives, including you."

"Does he remember his life on earth?" asks Hamza.

"Of course."

"He won't pray for me, then," says Hamza, flatly. 'The last he saw of me was my knee hitting him in the face."

☾

"The elders of Timbuktu are meeting tonight at the town hall," says Omar. "I overheard two of them talking about it at the market."

"Perfect," says Redbeard. "We will do our sunset prayers and then pay them all a visit."

Omar catches my eye. This is going to be interesting.

When we arrive at the town hall, we find a teenaged guard stationed outside the door, fiddling nervously with a slingshot and a whistle. As soon as he sees our guns, he hurries to let us in.

The tables in the meeting room are arranged in the form of a square. I recognize the mayor of Timbuktu, who sits at the top table. A bunch of plastic roses decorates the table before him, and a lazy fan revolves above his head. The other seats are occupied by older men. They stare like sheep as we burst into their meeting room and spread out along the walls, our rifles at the ready.

As soon as we are in position, Redbeard strides in, clasping his hands in front of him in an exaggerated show of respect. "Peace be upon you all!" he cries, Kalashnikov dangling at his side.

The whitebeards shift in their seats. Not one of them returns the greeting.

Redbeard makes his way into the center of the room and wags his index finger at the elders like a schoolteacher scolding his class. "Sura An-Nisa verse eighty-six," he says. "When you are accosted with a greeting of peace, answer with an even better greeting, or at least with the like thereof. For truly, God keeps count of all things."

I feel a surge of joy. Already Redbeard is on top. Already his purity of heart and his knowledge of the Book have flooded this dingy meeting room with the light of God.

The first elder to find his tongue is Imam Cissé. I recognize him from my childhood visits to the city.

"Peace be upon you, Ould," he mutters. "What are you doing here?"

"Cissé!" cries Redbeard, feigning surprise. "It has been a long time."

"Not nearly long enough," shoots back the imam. "What is it you want?"

"The same thing I've always wanted," says Redbeard. "I want to preach in Timbuktu. I want to teach God's Word. I want people to repent of their dissolution and doublemindedness. I want us all to walk soberly in the light of God. I want bars closed, cigarettes banned, women veiled, and schools reformed. I want Timbuktu to become what it used to be: a light to the nations, a center of scholarship, piety, and jihad."

"*Amen*," I whisper.

"Timbuktu is already a Muslim city," says the imam. "Don't make me lecture you in history, Ould."

"Leave your Qur'an unopened on the shelf," replies Redbeard, "and termites will devour it from the inside. Timbuktu looks Muslim from the outside, I grant you, but here at its heart, there is nothing but rot."

"I agree, we have work to do," says the imam. "We must encourage our people in the path of piety."

Redbeard shrugs his shoulders. "If the blind lead the blind, they will both fall into a pit."

"Ould Hamaha!" splutters the mayor. "How dare you insult our religious leaders?"

"Your religious leaders are practicing a false religion," Redbeard fires back. He moves across to the mayor's table and thumps it with both fists. "Let me tell you, Monsieur Mayor, what I saw on my way here tonight. Three women at a mud-brick tomb, praying to a saint for food: 'For daily salt we beg thee, Sidi Ahmed ben Amar . . .'"

"Visiting the tombs of the saints is a common—"

"Did you not hear me?" cries Redbeard. "*They were praying not to God himself but to a pile of bones!* Are you so blind that you cannot see what these flab-chinned imams have done to your city? Their idolatry is a stench in God's nostrils!"

"I disagree," says the mayor. "Sidi Ahmed was a wonder-ful—"

"Damn you!" Redbeard seizes the plastic flowers from the mayor's table and hurls them at the wall. "Sidi Ahmed was a man, and nothing more. A walking, talking, eating, sleeping, farting son of Adam. And if any imam in Timbuktu teaches his people to pray to Sidi Ahmed, I will throw him from a minaret and leave his body in the street for the dogs to eat."

A line has been crossed, and everybody knows it. The white-beards are staring at Redbeard in horror. Omar and Jabir, across the room from me, are gaping like snapper fish. But our master is right to use strong words. Nothing in this world is more despi-cable than idolatry.

"Let us not fight," says Redbeard, smiling suddenly. "Since Imam Cissé obviously distrusts me, I would like to prove my good faith by accepting one of his daughters in marriage."

There follows another awkward silence. My master is out of his mind to suggest that.

"Are you serious?" asks the mayor. "You threaten our imam with death and then you ask to marry his daughter?"

"Any of your daughters," beams Redbeard. "It makes no difference to me, provided she is a virgin. Now that I have come back to Timbuktu, I feel obliged to—"

"You have not come back to Timbuktu!" cries Imam Cissé, jumping to his feet. "Timbuktu has seven gates: tolerance, honor, dignity, generosity, hospitality, honesty, and justice. Gunpowder and grenades are not gates to Timbuktu. You want to marry an elder's daughter? You would more easily swallow the moon."

Redbeard looks at the old man and smiles. It is a strange sort of smile, involving the lips, but not the eyes. "I did not expect your love," he says, "but neither did I expect insults. Thank you, Imam Cissé. You have given me occasion to follow the example of the Prophet, peace be upon him. He was insulted, cursed, and struck with fists, but he never once—"

"Don't talk of him!" cries the imam. "Do not sully his name. Go back to the desert and to your camels, you hideous, straggle-beard son of a—"

The imam's rant is silenced by a soft metallic click. Redbeard has flicked off the safety catch of his AK-47.

"Good night, old men," says Redbeard. "I had hoped to discuss with you some of the changes that will be introduced by the new regime, but I see you are not ready. You will hear them on the radio tonight, along with everybody else in this wretched town."

Redbeard turns on his heel and leaves. In single file we follow him outside. "It is early days," he tells us. "Those old men are blinded by their fear and pride, so they cannot recognize the beauty of our ideas. But soon they will understand, and Timbuktu will shine again like a jewel in the desert's crown."

Occupation needs organization, says Redbeard. He gives a

task to every member of the battalion, and entrusts the Ninjas with night patrol. We are to walk the streets of Timbuktu from sunset to sunrise, quashing rebellion and enforcing sharia.

Askia is mine. It is a long, dusty street that stretches from the Ahmad Baba Library in the north all the way down to Independence Square in the south. Near the top of the street is the Djinguereber Mosque with its rose-red ramparts and minarets. Farther down toward the square stand two elegant villas with whitewashed mud-brick walls, arched entrances, and sculpted balustrades.

After sunset prayer at the military camp, I start my patrol. The avenue is deserted, save for some stray dogs snarling and scrapping by the west wall of the mosque. Up and down, up and down, I hobble on my crutches, until my underarms are as sore as my ankle.

At eight o'clock my phone alarm goes off. Time for Redbeard's broadcast.

A ramshackle mechanic's workshop stands opposite the whitewashed villas, and beside the workshop lies a huge discarded tractor tire. I sit down on the tire, rest my AK-47 on my lap, and engage the radio function on my phone. It crackles for a minute and then Redbeard's strident voice comes on, addressing us with holy zeal.

Praise be to Allah, Lord of the worlds, the Merciful, the Compassionate.

Peace be upon you all.

Timbuktu has been liberated from the grasp of infidels, and reclaims its rightful heritage as a beacon of Islam.

We have appointed Muhammad Zaarib to enforce sharia in the commune of Timbuktu. He is well versed in all aspects of sharia and is not afraid to punish transgressors.

We advise all residents of Timbuktu to take note of the following laws:

Do not permit your wives and daughters to appear in public with their heads or bodies uncovered. In Timbuktu, females above the age of ten must wear the veil in accordance with the instruction of the Prophet, peace be upon him. Women who appear in public without a veil will receive twenty lashes with a camel-hide whip.

Men should wear long shirts and baggy trousers cut well above the ankle.

Women must not walk or talk with men in public. In Timbuktu, any woman caught consorting with a man will receive twenty lashes with a camel-hide whip.

Do not smoke harmful substances. The Prophet himself, peace be upon him, said that whomsoever drinks poison, thereby killing himself, will sip this poison forever in the fire of Hell. Cigarettes are haram. *Anyone who sells them in Timbuktu will be punished with twenty lashes.*

Do not listen to music, for it intoxicates the heart and weakens the body. The Prophet, peace be upon him, warned his followers of a day when Muslims would proclaim fornication and the playing of musical instruments legal. Not so in Timbuktu! Anyone who plays or listens to music will receive twenty lashes with a camel-hide whip.

Do not frequent bars, for they are quagmires of sin. Do not drink beer or other alcoholic drinks, not even at home, for they are haram, *forbidden. All bars and nightclubs in Timbuktu must close their doors forever, and anyone who sells the devil's brew will be punished with forty lashes.*

Do not wear amulets around your neck. Amulets divert the heart from putting its trust in God. And do not hang amulets on your children, for this creates more fear than it allays. Marabouts who write amulets and leatherworkers who sew amulet pouches will be punished with twenty lashes.

Do not watch television or listen to the radio. These appliances are a waste of time at best. At worst they are agents of depravity and debauchery. Your mind belongs to God. Stop polluting it with needless chatter and hateful images. As soon as this broadcast finishes, place your radio in a pounding pot and pound it to fine dust. If you own a television, drop it from a rooftop. Break these Satans beyond repair and vow instead to pursue purity with all your heart. After this broadcast, anyone caught watching television or listening to a radio will receive twenty lashes with a camel-hide whip.

Do not steal, for stealing is a crime against both God and man. In Timbuktu, anyone caught stealing will have his right hand amputated at the wrist.

Do not commit fornication. Anyone who commits fornication will be punished with one hundred lashes.

Do not commit adultery. In Timbuktu, anyone who commits adultery will be put to death.

As a service to the commune of Timbuktu, Muhammad Zaarib will enforce these laws. Purify yourselves of all unrighteousness and support the police in their noble task.

Praise be to Allah, Lord of the worlds, the Merciful, the Compassionate.

This is the end of the broadcast. Peace be upon you all. Smash your radios.

I sit on my tire and gaze at the sky in the east. Ali the warrior is rising over the rooftops, and with him rises a new era of faith, hope, and purity in Timbuktu. I will not smash my phone—I need it for work—but in the morning I will ask Omar to disable the radio function. We are the Defenders of Faith, and we must set a good example.

☽

The coal-black sky turns indigo, then gray. Lying across the tractor tire, I nurse my painful underarms and watch the vultures passing overhead.

When my gaze returns to earth, I see a girl sitting on a stool outside the villa opposite. She is wearing a patterned, wrap-around skirt and her hair stands up around her head in a crown of spikes. She is muttering under her breath as she reads from the manuscript on her lap.

I hobble across the street on my crutches and a divine aroma greets me: oleander flowers and fresh milk.

"You should be veiled," I tell the girl in French. "Did you not hear us on the radio last night? In Timbuktu, females above the age of ten must wear veils, and those who appear in public without veils will receive twenty—"

She looks lazily up from her manuscript. "I'm not allowed to talk with men," she says. "Or boys," she adds pointedly.

"This is not talking," I say. 'This is a police matter."

"*Une affaire de police*," she corrects me. "*Affaire* is feminine."

"What is your name?"

"Kadi Diallo."

"Where is your veil?"

"I don't own one."

"That's no excuse. When the verse of the veil was first revealed to the Prophet, peace be upon him, the women of Mecca tore their skirts in their haste to cover their faces."

She laughs abruptly, although I haven't made a joke. Then she looks at me more closely, studying my features.

"What's wrong?" I say.

"You're from the Fulani tribe," she says. "I can tell by the shape of your nose, and that little gap between your front teeth. I would guess that this time last year you were herding your father's cows out in the bush, like a good Fulani boy, walking for kilometers and kilometers and—" She cocks her head to one side and frowns. "Or have you always been lame?"

"I'm not lame. I'm injured."

"You should drink milk," she says. "It strengthens your bones. I can get you milk, if you have money."

"I don't need milk."

"A Fulani boy who doesn't need milk!" She raises her eyebrows. "What have your Arab masters done to you?"

She is confident, this girl, and disrespectful too.

"God alone is my master," I tell her. "And in public, females above the age of ten must wear—"

"This isn't public. This is the porch of my own house."

"It's the street."

She lifts her stool, moves it backward a meter, and grins at me. "Now it's the porch."

She thinks she's clever. She's laughing at me and at the new regime. Just because I'm roughly her age, she thinks she can get away with anything.

"I'm Fulani too," she grins. "But I suppose you guessed that already, from the way my hair is braided."

"Your hair should not be showing at all," I snap. "Get a veil!"

I put my weight back on my crutches and hobble across the street. When I reach the other side of the street, she holds up her book and quotes in a loud voice. "'Prince Sundiata was a sickly creature. Even at seven years old, the boy still crawled, spent all his time eating, and had no friends. His mother's co-wives mocked him. "Are you a lion or a louse?" they asked.'"

I turn and point the end of my crutch at her. "'*Beware*,'" I quote, "'*for the lion will walk and then he will pounce.*'"

"You've read the epic of Sundiata!" Her face lights up.

"Of course," I reply. "And that manuscript you're holding is in Arabic, so it's clearly not the epic of Sundiata. Don't take me for a fool, Kadi."

"Kadija!" she calls after a long pause. "Only my friends call me Kadi."

"Get a veil," I shout back, "or I'll bring you one myself!"

I swing along the street toward the Djinguereber Mosque, the ends of the crutches digging painfully into my armpits.

I'll bring you one myself.

Why did I have to say that? Just when I was winning, I had to go and spoil it all.

☾

After two o'clock afternoon prayers, Redbeard summons the whole battalion. He stands on the tailgate of his truck, a black turban loosely wound round his forehead. 'The Prophet, peace be upon him, cursed ten people with regard to alcohol. Who can list these unfortunate souls?"

Omar's hand shoots up. 'The one who makes it," he gabbles, "the one for whom it is made, the one who drinks it, the one who carries it, the one to whom it is carried, the one who pours it, the one who sells it, the one who consumes its price, the one who buys it, and the one for whom it is bought."

"Good," says Redbeard, and the light of God blazes in his eyes. "That means every son of Adam and Eve in this miserable city is under a curse. They call it the city of three hundred and thirty-three saints, but in truth it is the city of three hundred and thirty-three bars!"

Titters of laughter.

"When the Prophet arrived in Mecca with his companions, peace be upon them, that city also labored under the curse of idolatry. How did he respond? Did he speak softly to the people? Did he reason and plead? No! He roamed the streets, he raged

61

against the idols, and he smashed them up!"

Redbeard's hands thrash the air. Spittle flies from the corners of his mouth. One end of his turban is dangling at his waist, but he neither sees nor cares. This is a man on a mission, a man consumed by love for Timbuktu and hatred of the evils that enslave its people. Under his spiritual leadership, the city of Timbuktu has a glorious future.

"Beer and spirits are the idols of Timbuktu," he thunders. "Let the blood run hot in your arteries, boys, and rage against the idols. Close down every bar, nightclub, cabaret, and liquor kiosk, and smash any televisions or musical instruments that you see on the way. Go in God's name and clean up this filthy town."

He splits the battalion into ten platoons and appoints a commander for each one. I am to lead Omar, Jabir, and Hamza. We sling our AK-47s across our bodies and recite Al-Fatiha.

"You should appoint a deputy," Hamza tells me as we make our way out of the compound.

"Why?"

"In case anything happens to you." Hamza curls his lip. "Like last time."

Like last time. I want to grab him by the scruff of his shirt and demand what he means by that. I want to make him admit, loud and clear, that he blames me for his brother's death. But doing that would shame us both.

"You be my deputy," I tell him. "You're brave, like your brother was."

Baba Bar on Toumani Avenue is open for business, so we walk right in. The owner cowers behind the counter as we raise our guns, open fire, and strobe the liquor shelf from end to end. The air twinkles with flying glass. Forbidden liquids run down the wall and flow in rivulets across the tiled floor. My nostrils fill with the aniseed stench of *pastis* liquor.

I love this sound of exploding bottles. It is the sound of purity and wisdom, the sound of God returning to Timbuktu.

"Watch this," I tell the others.

I bend down to a pool of alcohol on the floor and fire at an angle. The muzzle flash from my rifle sets fire to the spirits, and a light blue flame licks across the floor and up the walls. It makes a dry, sipping sound, like a Tuareg sucking the last drops of tea out of a glass.

The owner of the bar emerges from behind the counter and dances to safety across the fiery floor. As of this moment, Baba Bar is closed. Its wooden counter and wicker chairs will burn bright all afternoon.

The next bar on Toumani Avenue is Calypso. The cattle herders in my village love this place. On market days they come to Timbuktu, and if they succeed in selling a cow or two they come to Calypso afterward to tip forbidden liquids down their throats. Poor souls! If only Redbeard would come and preach in my village, the herders would repent and join our cause, I know they would.

There are no forbidden liquids on the shelves, but there are posters of soccer players all over the walls. Samuel Eto'o, Yaya Touré, Didier Drogba. These too are idols. Redbeard says that all those who play or watch soccer will regret it in the afterlife. Spheres of granite the exact size of soccer balls will fall on their heads from a great height.

In the sandy yard behind the bar we find a tower of beer crates as high as a camel. Beside the beer crates is a deep hole.

"Nice day for burying beer!" I call.

A man and a boy stare up at us from the bottom of the hole.

They are holding spades and their T-shirts are damp with sweat.

"Beer is forbidden," I tell them. "You are not supposed to hide it. You are supposed to destroy it."

They climb up out of the hole and start to dismantle the tower of beer crates. They smash the bottles with their spades, and shovel the broken glass into the hole.

"Peace be upon you," I say, when the job is done. "If another bottle of beer crosses the threshold of your house, you will both receive forty lashes."

Our next stop is the famous La Détente nightclub. The name La Détente is famous nationwide; all of Mali's best-known artists have played here.

Parked outside the club is a moto-taxi, a Chinese motorbike bolted to a three-wheeled trailer. A boy with long hair is sitting sideways on the saddle, smoking. When he sees us coming, he whips the cigarette out of his mouth and throws it on the ground.

"Got any more of those?" I ask him.

He shakes his head.

"Lighter?"

He hands it over.

"Cigarettes are *haram*, forbidden," I say. "If I catch you smoking again, I'll have you whipped."

We go into the club. There are chairs and tables all around, with empty wine bottles for candleholders. An old, gas-powered fridge stands in the corner. Black-and-white photos of musicians cover the walls.

Back in my herding days, I listened to music all the time. I walked behind my cows with my pocket radio pressed to my ear, my spirit soaring to the tunes of Ali Farka Touré, Salif Keita, and Kandia Kouyaté. My mind would stray, and my cows would stray too, usually into someone's millet field. Which meant that my father had to pay compensation to many farmers. Which meant he would beat me fiercely with a birch branch. Last year, when I first heard Redbeard preach about music, I realized straightaway how right he was. That same night I put my radio in my mother's pounding pot and smashed it to a glinting grit.

Behind the bar I find a dog-eared sheet of paper—a list of names and telephone numbers of musicians who use the club. Troublemakers.

Jabir comes in and sniffs the air. "What's that smell?" he asks.

"Dust." Omar runs a fingertip across one of the tables. "And stale cigarette smoke."

And oleander, I think. And milk.

I wander over to the stage. Like everything else, it is covered with thick dust, and like all dust, it tells a story. The rectangle of a balaphone, the circle of a djembe drum, a smattering of recent footprints. Three people were here not long ago, retrieving musical instruments. The balls of their feet have left clearer impressions than the heels, which means they were in a hurry.

The only things remaining on the stage are five low stools belonging to the club. How many of my former idols, I wonder, have sat on those stools to weave their magic?

Former idols. The words stir me. *Let the blood run hot in your arteries, boys, and rage against the idols.* I take taxi boy's lighter out of my pocket, flick it open, and light the candle on the table in front of me. In a waking dream, I move from table to table, lighting the other candles one by one.

"What are you doing?" asks Jabir.

"Closing down the club," I say.

When all the candles are lit, I go over to the gas-powered fridge, disconnect the butane bottle, and drag it into the middle of the floor. I can tell by the weight that the bottle is nearly full.

Omar is the first to realize what I am doing. "No," he says, rushing over to me. "This is not like those other bars. This is La Détente."

"Exactly. That's why we have to make an example of it."

"What's going on?" asks Jabir.

"He's going to puncture the cylinder," says Omar. "The depressurized butane liquid will vaporize into a massive, white gas cloud, which will then ignite on the candles."

"You mean, it will explode?"

"Explode isn't the word," says Omar. "It will scatter pieces of La Détente across the whole Sahara."

"I'll do it," says Hamza quickly, and we turn to look at him. "One bullet is all it will take."

It is the first thing Hamza has said all afternoon.

"Wait for my order," I tell him, heading toward the swinging doors at the back of the club. "I'll check that there is no one out back."

In the yard behind La Détente there are more tables, a broken amplifier, and a row of tall clay water jars. The oleander scent is stronger here.

"Peace be upon you, Kadija!" I call.

She comes out from behind the water jars, clasping a djembe drum in her arms. "And upon you," she mutters.

"I saw your footprints inside, all three of you. Where are the others?"

A shame-faced, short-haired girl and skinny boy emerge from behind the water jars, with a kora and a ngoni in their hands.

"Musical instruments are forbidden," I tell them. "They distract the mind and pollute the—get down!"

A single shot and telltale hiss of gas have alerted me. They are followed by a bone-shaking explosion. There is heat and dust and hellish noise and the wall behind me collapses to the ground.

☾

I am lying still, surrounded by rubble, ears ringing painfully. Kadija is right in front of me, her hair and face caked with dust. She's alive, and still holding her drum. If she had been wearing a veil, she would have stayed clean as well. God knows best.

We lie looking at each other. Kadija says something to me, which I can't make out. She gets up, wincing, and picks her way past me across the rubble, clasping the djembe awkwardly in front of her.

"Stop!" I shout. "Put that drum down!"

The roof of La Détente has collapsed, and two of its walls as well. Tables and candles and photos of idols are buried under tons of masonry. As of this moment, the club is closed.

The skinny boy and short-haired girl are also on their feet. They brush the debris off their clothes, pick up their *haram* instruments, and follow Kadija down a narrow alleyway along the west side of the building, where the wall of the club is still intact.

"Omar!" I yell. "West side, Omar!"

I stand my crutches upright on the ground, pull myself to my feet, and propel myself as fast as I can along the alleyway. The engine of a motorbike sputters alive, and I realize that the moto-taxi we ignored outside is in fact a getaway vehicle.

God be praised, when I reach the street the taxi is still there. The instruments are piled up in the trailer and the miscreants are standing with their hands above their heads, staring down the barrels of three AK-47s. Poor kids.

"Are you all right?" Hamza asks me, and there is a strange half smile on his face.

"Of course I'm not!" I shout. "I told you to wait for my order!

You could have killed me!"

Hamza gazes back at me with empty eyes. That's it, I realize. That's exactly what he wanted to do.

The girl with the short hair is furious too. "Look at it!" she says, pointing with her chin at the ruins of La Détente. "Look what you have done!"

"I know," says Hamza. "I don't think Salif Keita will be playing here tonight, do you?"

I swing myself over to the moto-taxi, take out the instruments, and throw them on the ground.

Kadi's lower lip is trembling. "Leave those alone," she says in a small voice. "They're the only ones we've got."

I stand over the kora and raise one of my crutches high into the air.

"*Saabe Allah*," whispers Kadi. For God's sake. She is pleading with me in our mother tongue, and there is no longer any trace of sarcasm in her voice.

"This *is* for God's sake," I tell her. "One day you will understand."

I bring down my crutch as hard as I can onto the kora. The bowl-shaped body breaks into three pieces and the goatskin splits from side to side.

The short-haired girl emits a howl of pain. "That's mine!" she screams. "What are you doing?"

"The will of God," I answer, swinging the crutch a second time. This time the notched bridge caves in and the rosewood neck snaps in two. Strings fly apart with twangs of tortured dissonance.

Kadi's friend throws herself at me, hammering my chest with her fists, and reaching up to scratch my face. The skinny boy jumps forward and pulls her off me.

"Aisha, no," he says.

I pick up the four-stringed ngoni. "Is this yours?" I ask the boy. He nods.

"Smash it yourself," I tell him.

His knees are shaking as he takes his precious instrument and dashes it against the ground. The neat, canoe-shaped body cracks in half and the rosewood handle snaps.

"*Nyammu inna maa*," mutters Kadi, in a peculiar throaty voice.

I ignore the insult and turn my attention to the djembe drum. Projecting all my love for God into a fierce, hard ball in my right hand, I punch down onto, and through, the tight skin of the djembe. Then I use the fuel line from the engine of the moto-taxi to spray the broken instruments with gasoline.

The skinny boy is staring dull-eyed at the broken instruments. The girls are sobbing.

I take the taxi boy's lighter from my pocket, flick it open, and hold the flame in the air. Symbols are important, Redbeard likes to say. When we deal with stubborn, godless people, we must make our point in a way they will never forget.

"*Do not listen to music, for it intoxicates the heart and weakens the body*," I quote. "*The Prophet, peace be upon him, warned his followers of a day when parts of the Muslim community would proclaim fornication and the playing of musical instruments legal. Not so in Timbuktu!*"

I bend down to torch the instruments, and grateful flames leap up toward the sky.

When the fire is blazing well, I notice a stray kora string and two small metal rivets lying on the sand.

"Keep these as a souvenir," I tell the short-haired girl, handing them to her. "God does not want your music. He wants your heart."

☾

That night, Redbeard visits the Djinguereber Mosque. He says he wants our platoon to go with him as bodyguards. He too is calling us the Ninjas. When the Tuaregs called us that, I got annoyed, but from Redbeard it's all right.

"*Kok, kok*!" calls Redbeard when we arrive in the sandy courtyard of the mosque. "Anybody here?"

Imam Karim emerges from his mosque and glares at us with undisguised loathing. "What do you want, Ould Hamaha?" he says.

"Peace be upon you too," says Redbeard. "I have come to ask you for a favor. My men and I would like to use your mosque for Friday prayers."

The imam shakes his head. "Out of the question. There is no room."

Redbeard's eyes darken. "Of course," he says. "I had forgotten. I hear that on certain days your mosque can be quite a crush."

Did he just say that? Did my master really just say that? I close my eyes and I am back there in an instant: the dust, the noise, the screams, the pressure on my ribs, the fight to breathe. That poor young garibou in front of me, big eyed, blue lipped: *Wallam*. Help me.

I open my eyes and see the old imam clutching his heart and struggling for breath himself. "How dare you?" he gasps. "How dare you?" He stands there with watering eyes and quivering jowls, and then—I have seen many strange things, but none so strange as this—he gets down on his knees and spreads himself prostrate on the sand.

It is Redbeard's turn to be shocked, but he disguises his confusion with a laugh. "What are you doing?" he says. "Are you sick?"

"God be praised, I am not sick," replies the imam. "Bogga!"

he calls. "Bring me cool water."

A mosque steward hurries to a clay pot on the edge of the courtyard and fills a large goblet with water. He offers it to the imam, who shakes his head.

"Pour it on my head," says Imam Karim.

The steward hesitates.

"Do it," says the imam quietly.

The cold water splashes over the old man's beard and down his neck, making him gasp and shiver.

"You've gone mad," says Redbeard. "Either that or you are possessed by a djinni."

The imam turns his face to the ground and starts to chant in Arabic. *"O son! Seek refuge from anger in God. When you get angry, lie down! If necessary, pour cold water on yourself."*

"Shameful," mutters Redbeard. "I would not pray in this mosque if you begged me to, not for all the salt in the Sahara."

Redbeard turns and stalks out into the street. With heavy hearts, we Ninjas follow him. We leave the ancient imam lying soggy and victorious in the middle of the courtyard of his mosque.

☾

I patrol Askia all through the night, hobbling up and down the empty street. Each time I pass the Djinguereber Mosque I think of the sodden imam on the sand, and each time I pass Kadi's house I hear the sound of weeping from the roof.

When midnight comes I wash my ears and feet and do Tahajjud, the optional midnight prayer.

I pray in my own words, as Redbeard taught me to. I pray that God will forgive Redbeard for his rash words in the mosque, and that He will stop Kadi feeling sad. He can do that, I know He can. He can show her that she is better off without her instruments.

☾

On my way back to camp the next morning, Redbeard's Land Cruiser stops and picks me up. I hop into the trailer to join my friends.

"Where are we going?" I ask.

"Airport," says Jabir. "We are visiting Chief Litni."

It's a real squash in the trailer this morning, because a huge machine gun has been mounted in the middle.

"Gift from Libya," Omar explains. "We've got eleven of these things, enough for all the trucks."

"Does anyone know how to fire it?"

"Only Redbeard. He's going to teach us when he has the time."

When we arrive at the airport, we see the flag of Azawad flying from the roof: a complex design of green, red, yellow, white, and black.

The chief is sitting in the parking lot, surrounded by advisors. They are reclining on wicker chairs, and three of them have teapots bubbling at their feet.

"Peace be upon you, Litni," says Redbeard, getting out of the car.

Chief Litni reaches forward, lifts the lid of his teapot, and adds six cubes of sugar to his brew. Only then does he acknowledge Redbeard's presence.

"And you," he mutters.

"I got the shopping list you sent me," says Redbeard. "Handgun rounds, machine gun cartridges, mortars, rockets. It seems you are out of almost everything."

Litni takes a cigarette from his pocket and lights up. "As you know, we have fought hard."

"And you really have nothing left?"

"A few handgun rounds," says Litni.

"What about fuel for the vehicles?"

"No problem. Fuel is the one thing we do have."

"Excellent," beams Redbeard. "In that case, you and your men will leave Timbuktu this afternoon."

Chief Litni takes two small tea glasses from a silver tray at his feet and rinses them out. When at last he speaks, his voice is tense.

"We like Timbuktu," he says. "The streets are clean. The girls are pretty. The tea and sugar are free. We intend to remain here for a very long time."

Redbeard, still smiling, shakes his head. "You will leave by sunset."

The Tuareg chief leaps to his feet. "Who took Timbuktu? Who took the military camp, the radio station, and the airport? One hundred and fifty Tuareg freedom fighters, that's who, and only ten of your men!"

"We funded your godless group because you were useful," says Redbeard. "You are useful no longer."

"Then we will fight you," snarls Litni.

"With no ammunition," shoots back Redbeard. "I look forward to that."

Litni's jaw clenches under his turban. Hatred smolders in his eyes. "We Tuareg have a proverb," he snarls. "*When you drive out a mouse, be sure to cover all its holes.* I will come back with many men, Ould Hamaha. More men than you can imagine."

"Men don't win wars," says Redbeard. "Money does. Our mission has many rich backers in Saudi Arabia, and not one of them cares a fennec fart for Azawad. Farewell, Litni."

He walks back to the vehicle and climbs in.

Sitting next to me in the tray, Jabir pulls a fold of his turban up over his mouth. His shoulders are shaking, he's trying so hard not to laugh.

Redbeard starts to drive away, then stops and winds down the window. "One more thing, Litni!" he shouts, pointing up at the roof of the airport. "When you get back to your sand dune, tell your wife to redesign the Azawad flag. Tell her it's an eyesore. Too many colors by half."

Manuscript 2,746

One day, Imam Malik was asked forty-eight questions about God.
He answered thirty-two of those questions with the words "I don't know."

Kadija

Eight kilometers north of Timbuktu, a gnarled, old rosewood tree stands in the desert. I am lying under the tree with my head in Aisha's lap. A mellow fragrance emanates from the bucket at my side, which brims with oleander petals. It should be more than enough for a bottle of perfume.

It has been a good morning. First we found the oleander bush, and then, a few kilometers on, we found this rosewood tree and cut a handsome branch for the neck of Aisha's new kora.

"Do you think the kora will be ready in time for Tondi's wedding?" I ask.

"I don't know," she says. "Newborn koras are terrible at holding their pitch. Ten days might not be enough."

"You can retune the strings between each song, if you need to."

Aisha nods and twirls the rosewood stick between her fingers. "Whose yard should we use for the ceremony?"

"I don't know. The Defenders of Faith have eyes and ears

76

everywhere. There's not a single street in Timbuktu they don't patrol."

"That's that, then," says Aisha. "There's no point making a new kora if your Fulani friend comes along and smashes it the minute I start to play."

"He's not my friend," I snap. "Don't call him that."

"He sent you a veil, didn't he?"

"Only one of those cheap, clingy ones."

"Will you wear it?"

"Of course not. Marimba can wear it at night when the cold season arrives."

Aisha throws back her head and laughs, displaying the peculiar necklace across her smooth black throat. It is the string from her smashed kora, with two silver rivets hanging from it like tiny pendants.

I reach up to touch it. "How long are you going to wear this thing?"

"Not long," she says. "I'll use it to slit the Fulani's throat, and then I'll stop wearing it." She reaches for a handful of oleander petals and crushes them in her palm. "The worst bit for me was when he started spraying gasoline around. As if smashing the instruments to pieces wasn't enough for him."

"The worst for me," I say, "was the club being blown up. It happened so fast, and I was lying there with those great slabs of concrete falling all around, terrified that one of them would fall on me." I gaze up at the pale, triangular foliage above our heads and change the subject quickly. "My uncle's sheep love rosewood leaves. We should gather some to take home with us."

"I'm too tired," Aisha murmurs, stroking my hair. "Besides, we're not going back to Timbuktu. We'll stay right here all day and all night."

"Really? What will we eat?"

"We'll eat your oleander petals."

"Ha! Do you know how poisonous they are? We'll be dead before sunrise!"

"So much the better."

She is talking crazy, but I do know how she feels. Here in the desert we can walk unveiled without fear of arrest. We can laugh, we can sing, we can do anything. We are free.

I scramble to my feet.

"Fire ants?" asks Aisha.

"No, I've had an idea. We'll celebrate Tondi's wedding right here. We can make as much noise as we like and no one will disturb us."

"Are you serious? A wedding in the desert?"

"It will be romantic." I stride out into the sunlight, imagining the scene. "The wedding hut will be over there, and we can play our music right here under the rosewood tree."

Aisha claps her hands. "Tondi will love it!" she cries. "And my new kora will love it too. She will sing all the sweeter if she knows her mother-tree is listening."

༄

That night, I lie on my mat on the edge of the roof, peering between the limestone balusters. A lonely figure is making his way along the road toward our house. I recognize him by his limp when he is still a long way off. It's the Fulani fanatic, the one who burned our instruments. The one who Aisha wants to kill. The one she called my friend.

Some friend!

He wends his painful way toward the tractor tire, his favorite spot for passing the night. I hate him, but I cannot help wondering what he will do tonight to while away the hours.

Some nights he writes and recites.

Some nights he plays with a lemon-shaped ball, tossing it from hand to hand.

Some nights he takes a small knife from the sheath on his belt and whittles bits of wood into rice spoons or writing boards, sticking his tongue out as he concentrates.

Some nights he exercises with his toes braced under the rim of the tire. Sit. Lie. Sit. Lie. The muscles in his abdomen flex and pop with every repetition.

Some nights he performs Tahajjud. He must know that these midnight prayers are optional, but he does them all the same. Perhaps he senses that he is being watched.

☽

The night of Tondi's wedding has arrived, and I am standing under the rosewood tree, preparing to get possessed. To my left is the wedding hut. To my right are Aisha and the band. Before me is a crowd, mostly teenagers, desperate to party. Above me, rosewood leaves and stars.

Imam Cissé has lent us an amplifier and four microphones from the Sidi Yahya Mosque. Al Haji Maiga lent us his cattle truck to transport the guests, and he said we can use the truck's battery to power the amp. All of Timbuktu is praying that the wedding will go well. This party is the only resistance movement we have.

Our very first song will be "the political song," "Alla La Ke." It tells the story of two princes in a kingdom called Tumana. One brother stole the chieftaincy from the other and banished him from the land. Eventually the rightful heir returned and the chieftaincy was given back to him. The song is part of Mali's soul, and tonight it will speak to our spirits more than ever before. Hold fast, the song urges. You cannot force God's hand. A dark regime cannot last long. The reign of the wicked prince will pass.

Aisha sits with the kora between her knees and starts to pluck the intro. Raoul the drummer pounds the rhythm on a Fulani wedding drum, an upturned calabash gourd on a tray of water. The deep wet thud of the water calabash mingles with the twang of virgin kora strings and makes my skin tingle with pleasure. Then Yusuf's new ngoni comes in, crisp and rapid, loaded with cheeky cross-rhythms. Alpha's balaphone completes the tapestry of sound. It shimmers everywhere, subtle and mesmerizing. Each note glows.

I open my mouth and "Alla La Ke" rises from my abdomen.

> *"Man asks but God arranges.*
> *God wanted it this way.*
> *You can't change his laws,*
> *You simple mortal."*

A performer at the Festival of the Desert once gave me a piece of advice about singing. "Let the music overtake you," she said. "If you don't let it possess you, what chance does it have of touching anyone else? Sing like a minstrel. Dance like a dervish. Feel the rhythm of the balaphone in your toes and your pelvis and in the roots of your hair and along each fingernail. Don't worry how you look or sound. Just stand up there and get possessed."

A bridesmaid sails out of the crowd and twirls a path across the sand toward the calabash. Her orange dress and creamy sash whirl and flick round her form. Her flashing eyes and floating hair are splendidly unveiled.

As the final kora notes of "Alla La Ke" depart across the desert, I hear the sound of sobbing. By the light of the waning half moon, I can make out a horse's silhouette on the crest of a nearby dune. The man in the saddle wears a prayer hat and a wide-shouldered robe. Behind him sits a weeping girl.

A bride always weeps when she arrives at her wedding. There will be joy later on, but for now she dwells on her sadness. She weeps for her mother and father. She weeps for her siblings. She weeps for her lost childhood. And if she has no real tears to shed, she fakes it. *The tears of a bride are not the same as the tears of a hyena victim*, goes the proverb.

As the horse prances down the side of the dune, Tondi's weeping gets louder. The drummer slows down the calabash and pounds deep thuds of joy, which fill my chest until it wants to burst. I feel my phone vibrate against my thigh, but checking my messages is the last thing on my mind.

Aisha adjusts the tuning rings along her kora's neck and plucks another ancient melody.

> *"A word on the wind is gathering strength.*
> *The word is strong, the word is sweet,*
> *Much louder than the wolves of war.*
> *The word is* khaira—*peace."*

The horse's hooves have disturbed the dune. There comes an eerie, rumbling sound that swells to a boom and then a roar, the perfect backing track.

People throughout the crowd are opening up their throats and trilling their tongues against their palates. I press my back against the gnarled bark of the rosewood tree, brace my feet against the sand, and add my voice to the singing dunes and ululating girls.

The horse arrives in our midst, prancing and capering, responding to the rhythm of the calabash and the gentle tweaks of its reins. Tondi's father is one of the most skillful horsemen in Timbuktu and this is his moment. The crowd surges round the horse. The air is thick with dust and joy.

Again my phone vibrates against my thigh. Again I ignore it. The drummer switches rhythm, and the deep thuds of "Khaira" give way to the lilting patter of "Jam Naati." This is the song we have gathered to sing, the song so meaningful that it gives its name to the whole wedding ceremony.

> *"Peace has entered, woman has come.*
> *Peace has entered, beauty has come."*

The horse wheels and cavorts in the moonlight. Tondi is no longer weeping. She is grinning all over her face. The bridegroom's aunties raise their arms, lift her off the back of the horse, and bear her aloft toward the door of the wedding hut.

The water calabash is thumping hard. The whole crowd is dancing. I spread my arms wide and stick my bottom out behind me. I will dance for Tondi and for Timbuktu. I will dance away my fear.

Yusuf caresses the fishing-line strings of his ngoni. His fingers fly along the fretless neck. He is an enigma, this cousin of mine. In person he is painfully shy, the only tongue-tied minstrel in the whole of Mali. But underneath the shyness beats a powerful heart. Put a ngoni in his hands and he becomes a well of wild, mischievous harmony.

"You and Yusuf are a perfect match," my aunties always say. My mother is more realistic. "You could do worse."

It's true, I could do worse. I bend over double and shuffle my feet back and forth on the sand, faster and faster. My left hand brushes Yusuf's shoulder as he plays.

"What's going on?" says Yusuf.

"Nothing," I say, turning away from him and wiggling my hips. "Don't let me distract you."

"No, I mean, why is Alpha not playing?"

Oh.

It's true. The blind balaphonist has stopped. His mallets hang in midair.

"Alpha, what's wrong?" I hiss. "Why aren't you playing?"

"Land Cruiser," he says.

I strain my ears to listen. Yes, he's right. Beneath the hollow thud of the water calabash sounds the faraway throb of a Land Cruiser engine.

"It's coming this way," says Alpha.

"Is it them?"

"It must be. They've commandeered all the Land Cruisers in town, haven't they?"

The bridegroom's aunts are pushing Tondi through the doorway of the new grass hut, and she is pretending to resist. The official part of the ceremony is almost over, but a whole night of dancing lies before us.

"Maybe it's tourists," says Alpha.

"You know it's not tourists. There haven't been tourists in Timbuktu since the kidnappings last year."

Yusuf stands up and removes the jingle plate from the neck of his ngoni. "Let's go," he says.

He is right, of course. We have no choice.

The guests groan when I announce the end of the party, but they too understand the danger. Everyone has heard what happened to Baba Bar and La Détente. No one wants to be caught within a mile of a kora. They surge forward and help us pack up our instruments. One helps Alpha with the balaphone, another takes the amplifier, another disconnects the truck battery and hoists it onto his shoulders.

Tondi the bride emerges from the wedding hut and runs to join us.

"I'm sorry," I say, hugging her.

"Don't be," Tondi smiles, and clambers up into the back of the truck. "God is always good."

We can see the headlights of the Land Cruiser now, coming at us from the south a mile or two away. There are about fifteen of us in the back of the truck: the band, the bride, and some kids who came on foot. We are fully loaded but the engine is silent. Hulking and immobile, the truck waits on the sand, a mass of slumbering steel.

Most of the wedding guests came on their own motorbikes or camel carts. As soon as they finished loading our truck, they rode off fast into the dunes, assuming we would follow close behind. *So why are we still here?*

I peer round the side of the truck. The driver is down on the ground, leaning against the door of his cab.

"Get in and drive!" I yell at him. "What are you waiting for?"

He stares back at me. "Battery," he says. "We're still waiting for the battery."

My skin prickles.

"Aisha!" I cry. "The battery is missing! Who disconnected it from the amp?"

"I didn't see. It was too dark."

We jump down to the sand and gaze at the desert. The desert gazes back. Undulant sand, acacia trees, and rocky moonlit crags deride us with their emptiness. "Battery? What battery?" they cry.

"Someone's taken it," I say. "Quick, spread out and search!"

Yusuf and the others jump down from the truck and scatter

in all directions, scanning the horizon for a fugitive with a massive battery.

The Land Cruiser is less than a mile away now, careering toward us with its headlights on full beam, its engine screaming as it plows the sand.

As I watch, the lights slew to the left and halt suddenly. A jolt of unexpected hope. They're swamped in sand! They'll have to dig the wheels out.

The race is on for us to find that battery. I loosen my wraparound skirt and start to run.

Calm down, Kadi, I tell myself. You're Fulani. You don't go haring off into the desert without first examining the tracks.

I hurry to the rosewood tree and shine the backlight of my phone across the sand. There it is, the deep rectangular print where the truck battery had lain. A flurry of footprints lead from the spot, mostly toward the truck.

Most but not all. One set of prints leads off into the dunes.

"Over here!" I yell. "Come with me!" I start to follow the tracks. Yusuf and the others will soon catch up with me. Away from the shade of the rosewood tree, the fugitive's footprints show up in the moonlight, the print of the right foot deeper than the left. It seems whoever stole our battery has a limp.

It's him. It has to be.

The footprints lead to the edge of a wadi, a dry riverbed. I jump down into the soft sand and look for where the tracks pick up.

I sense a sudden movement underneath the overhanging bank. A figure dressed in black darts from the shadows into the moonlight, heaves his load—our battery!—onto his shoulder, and starts to run.

"No you don't!" I stagger after him across the sand.

With his bad ankle and his heavy load, the mujahid is no

match for me. I tackle him round the waist and yank him to the ground.

Yusuf and the others are coming. I can hear them up on the bank, yelling their heads off. "Where are they?" they are asking. "Can you see them?"

"Help!" I shout.

I try to wrestle the battery out of the mujahid's arms but he's holding on too tight. I cannot get it free.

Our drummer Raoul is the first to spot us. He leaps down into the wadi and runs at the mujahid, braids a-flying. The boy stands up, dodges Raoul's flailing fists, and unleashes a punch of his own, a strong blow to the bottom of Raoul's chin. Our hothead drummer hits the sand like a hundred-kilo sack of yams.

Yusuf and the other boys arrive. They spread out to surround the mujahid and close in slowly, cautiously.

He stands his ground, stock-still, and waits until they're near. He knocks down Yusuf with a well-timed elbow, another boy with a head butt, another with a spinning kick. He is well-trained, this boy, and brave as well.

But he ignores me at his peril. I wriggle over to where he stands and lash out hard at his weaker ankle.

The mujahid drops to the sand, and my friends fall on him with savage blows and kicks. He is curled up with his arms round his head.

"God!" he gasps, and then goes quiet.

"Enough!" I tell the others. "It's the battery we need!"

☾

The battery is back in its compartment and connected to the engine, but we are not safe yet. The Land Cruiser is out of the sand and back in the chase. Its headlights are on full beam, shining straight at us like furious twin suns.

The truck rumbles into life and moves off. We all wrap cotton scarves round our heads, leaving narrow slots for the eyes. We're outlaws and we know it.

A man with a megaphone leans out the window of the Land Cruiser. "This is the Defenders of Faith," he cries. "Stop your vehicle and turn off the engine."

Our truck gathers speed, its massive tires churning the fine Saharan sand. We're not stopping now, not for all the salt in Taoudenni.

Raoul the drummer is shouting in French. "Potato truck! Get the potato truck!"

"Shush." I lay a hand on his shoulder. "Try and rest. You got hit on the head."

The Land Cruiser is still gaining on us. It is less than twenty meters away, its wheels moving smoothly in our ruts. The machine gun on the back of the Land Cruiser is pointing our way, and it's manned.

"Find the canvas bag!" shouts Raoul. "There's a potato truck inside!"

"Be quiet, Raoul!"

"No, wait," says Alpha in my ear. "He's not saying *camion*, he's saying *cannon*!"

I realize Raoul's plan. Our crazy drummer brought a potato canon with him, just in case.

Right now it's all we have.

We are too squashed to move, but the message gets passed around the truck, and soon the odd-shaped canvas bag is found. Inside are two lengths of PVC tubing, a can of hairspray, and a load of sweet potatoes. One of the PVC tubes is short and fat, with a cap on the end and some sort of ignition mechanism built in. The other tube is narrower.

"Who's going to fire it?" asks Alpha.

Silence.

"I'll do it," I hear myself say. "I saw one fired once. I think I can remember how it's done."

I take the tubes, connect them end to end, and shove a sweet potato in the top. The barrel's sharpened rim slices off the excess potato so that it fits perfectly.

Yusuf puts a hand on my shoulder. "Are you sure, Kadi? That's a *machine gun* on the back of their truck."

"The gun is just for show," I say. 'They're trying to scare us."

"They're succeeding," mutters Yusuf.

Alpha passes me his dark glasses and a balaphone mallet. I put the glasses on and use the slender mallet to push the potato as far down the tube as it will go. Then I take the cap off the larger tube and spray hairspray into the chamber. I replace the cap, hoist the cannon to my shoulder, and flip Alpha's shades down over my eyes to protect them from the glare.

"Yusuf, hold me steady," I tell him.

Aiming at a spot just above the headlights, I flick my thumb against the ignition. A blaze of light shoots from the cannon's barrel, and a deafening bang assaults my ears. Yusuf and I sprawl on the floor of the truck.

"I heard breaking glass!" cries Alpha. "Good shot, Kadi."

"The headlights are getting farther away!" Aisha shouts. "You did it, Kadi. You stopped a Land Cruiser with a potato!"

I am lying on my back on top of Yusuf. "Are you OK, cousin?" I whisper.

"No," he croaks. "You shouldn't wear so much wire in your hair."

"Well, *you* shouldn't have pulled me down on top of you."

"It was the recoil!"

I roll off him, giggling.

As we travel back to Timbuktu, I take out my phone and glance at it. Two missed calls and four new messages, all from the same number. Now that I think about it, I do remember my phone vibrating while I sang.

> Stop the party, Kadija. Music is against God's law.
> Stop right now, Kadija, or I'm calling for backup.
> Kadija, they know about the party. Run.
> Kadi, run. I don't want to see you get hurt.

Even at night there are checkpoints on all the roads into Timbuktu. Al Haji's truck drops us off on the outskirts of town, and we walk home through the backstreets. Aisha is singing under her breath.

"I don't know what you're so happy about," I say to her. "You know they can have us lashed for what we did tonight?"

"They can't," she says. "Sharia says you need two witnesses to prosecute a crime. Your Fulani friend was on his own."

"Oi! Stop calling him my friend."

Some of the younger boys are walking in front of us, boasting about the fight. "Look how bruised my knuckles are!" says one. "I had him on the ground and I was punching him on the side of his head."

"I was kicking him," pipes up another. "Did you see me? I was kicking him in the ribs."

"And I lifted this off him," says a third, holding up a phone.

"Give me that!" I snatch the phone out of his hand. "Don't you realize there's a war going on for the soul of Timbuktu? Do you think that lifting phones is the way to fight that war?"

I pocket the phone and walk on.

☾

My parents are already asleep and snoring loudly. I fill a bucket from the water barrel and climb the tree-trunk staircase with the bucket on my head.

On the roof I get undressed and rinse the sand from between my toes. Midnight water is too cold for a full-bucket shower—I will bathe properly tomorrow.

I lie down under the stars, my mind whirling from the night's excitement. I count to a thousand, I even pray Tahajjud, but still I cannot sleep.

So instead I look at the mujahid's phone.

There are eight clips in the Videos folder.

The first two clips show an angry grizzled man standing on the back of a truck, preaching his beard off. Boring.

The third clip shows a group of boys playing high jump in the desert. One by one they fling themselves over a wooden bar and land on the sand with a forward roll. One boy lands on his head by mistake and the frame shakes wildly as the cameraman laughs. The boy jumps up and scowls into the lens in mock indignation.

The fourth is taken in low light and shows two fennec cubs play-fighting in the desert. They circle each other, bounce from side to side, and nibble on each other's ears.

The fifth shows the Fulani boy lying on his front on the crest of a dune. "Go with God, Ali," whispers a voice. "Think of your namesake at the Battle of Badr."

Ali. So that's his name.

The video zooms to focus on Ali as he sprints down the dune, leaps across a dry riverbed, and drops to a crouch at the foot of a concrete wall that rises incongruously out of the desert. He takes a grappling hook out of his satchel and—it's him! I'm sure of it! That Ninja Baba shot, it was Ali!

He must never find out who shot at him that night, I swear to myself. My father's safety is at stake.

I flick to the sixth video: Ali grinning stupidly next to a roasting goat.

The seventh clip shows two girls in the market, haggling for prawn crackers. Purity of God, he's been filming me and Aisha!

"How much for a bag of white men's ears?" my screen self asks the owner of the stall.

"Two hundred francs," comes the reply.

My screen self totters, gasps, and clutches Aisha's arm. 'Two hundred francs?" I cry. "We could get a bag of *real* white men's ears for that!"

I watch the video through three times. At first I am laughing, then I start to get annoyed. Judging by the swaths of printed cotton framing the video, the cameraman was hiding in a haberdasher's shack.

How dare he film me secretly!

The last video is also me. It is too dark to see much, but my voice is as clear as amber. "*Alla La Ke*," I'm howling to the moon. "*You can't change his laws, you simple mortal.*"

I drag my sleeping mat to the edge of the roof beside the balustrade. It's cooler there.

Sleep comes at last, but my dreams are laced with horror. During the night I wake four times and raise my head to look across the street, expecting to see Ali sitting on his tire.

It's empty every time.

Perhaps he's dead in the desert and vultures are feasting on his heart. That would be a sort of justice, I suppose. Those who try to rip out the desert's heart should expect the desert to rip out theirs.

Do I want him dead?

I don't know. He burned our instruments, but he also filmed those fennecs frolicking.

The jihadist loves animals. I suppose it's a start.

☪

The sun rises over Timbuktu.

I lift my head, and there he is, praise to the Lord of worlds, trying to do a sit-up on his tire. His broad chest is covered with dark bruises.

I tie my wraparound, fling a cotton shawl over my head, and scamper down the tree-trunk steps, out through the mud-brick entrance arch, and across the street. As I approach, he clambers off the tire and dons his shirt.

"You're back," I say.

He nods. One eye is swollen closed, and there are cuts on his face and chin.

"And are you going to have us lashed?"

He shakes his head. "Not enough witnesses."

So Aisha was right. I feel dizzy with relief, but I can't tell him that.

"You ruined our night" is all I say.

He squints at me through his good eye and the corner of his mouth twitches. "You ruined mine."

"How did you find out about the wedding?"

He shrugs. "You and I should not be talking."

"Do you want your phone back?"

"Not if it means I have to talk to you."

I feel a jolt of anger, but I press on. "You sent me some texts last night," I say. "Who gave you my number?"

"It was on a list at La Détente."

"You said you don't want to see me get hurt."

"That's right. I want to see you repent."

There it is again, that telltale quickening of my blood. I didn't come down here intending to get angry again, but I can't help it. "You want me to repent singing at a wedding? Do you really think that is a crime? Deep down, do you honestly believe God hates me singing at my friend's wedding?"

He winces and sits down on the edge of his tire. "Here's the thing, Kadi. Wherever music goes, sin follows. One minute you were singing, and a moment later you were wiggling your bottom in your boyfriend's face. There's a connection, don't you see?"

The blood in my cheeks runs hot. "That's a *traditional* dance I was doing."

"If you say so."

"And he's not my boyfriend."

"Like that makes it better!"

I stamp my foot and wave his phone in his face. "If you're such a saint, why have you been filming me and Aisha in secret?"

He bites his lip and looks away.

Got you.

"Intelligence gathering," he says at last. "We take videos of troublemakers and share them with our colleagues."

I throw the phone on the sand in front of him and stomp back across the street. "You're a toad!" I shout back. "I'm glad they beat you up."

☪

At two o'clock I go to the military camp with a calabash on my head. "Gift of milk for the mujahidin," I tell the sentry.

"It's prayer time," he says. "Wait here."

In the center of the compound, the Defenders of Faith are arrayed in lines, facing east, with that awful Redbeard man at the front. Some have their own prayer rugs. Others use rice sacks or T-shirts.

They stand and bow and kneel down, just like we do. They touch their foreheads on the sand, just like we do. Do they ever doubt themselves, these boys, or doubt their Arab master, or miss the love-drenched *dhikr* of their youth?

I lay down my calabash, pick up a longish twig, and pretend to stir my milk.

The sentry is praying too. If his forehead were not on the ground, he would see that there is not a single drop of milk in my calabash—just a phone. I position the end of the twig above the call button and press down.

Five seconds, four, three, two, one . . .

A burst of hard Ivorian rap explodes among the praying boys. *Come and swing your loppa-loppa! Swing your loppa all day long!*

Among the low curved backs a head pops up. The eyebrows arch. The mouth drops open.

It's saintly Ali, fumbling in his pockets. Not only did I change his ringtone, I set the volume as high as it would go. *Come and swing your loppa-loppa!* blares the rapper's song.

Redbeard unfolds. His eyes bulge, his beard quivers, and I have to press my veil across my mouth to stop myself laughing. This is even better than I'd hoped.

Ali can't get his phone out, not in that position. He jumps to his feet, treading on his neighbor's fingers.

"Ayeeee!" his neighbor squeals.

Come and swing your loppa-loppa! Swing your loppa all day long!

Several of the mujahidin have burst out laughing. There's hope for them yet, those boys. If "The Loppa-Loppa Song" can't make them laugh, what on God's earth can?

"Astaghfirullah!" cries Ali. "God forgive me!"

I'm guessing God's forgiveness is the easy bit. Redbeard's is another matter.

As I walk home up Askia Street, I phone Aisha and leave a voice mail. I am desperate to tell her what just happened, but I'm crying with laughter and can hardly put two words together. I just laugh like a lunatic until my credit runs out.

☾

That afternoon, my uncle pays a visit. I love Uncle Abdel because he talks to me in the same tone of voice that he uses with the elders. He is always asking my opinions on difficult subjects and recommending manuscripts for me to read.

"Good afternoon, Kadi," he says, shaking my hand. "Did you hear the news? The United Nations is refusing to recognize Azawad as an independent state. In their eyes, Kidal, Gao, and Timbuktu are still a part of Mali. What do you think of that?"

"At least they recognize that Timbuktu is a real place," I say.

My uncle's eyes crinkle at the corners and he chuckles into the folds of his turban.

"Seriously, though," I say, "Azawad is irrelevant right now. I'd rather hear what the UN is saying about Redbeard's force."

"Nothing yet," he says. "Diplomacy takes time. Tell me something, Kadi. Do you think the people of Timbuktu are doing enough to resist the occupation?"

"Not nearly enough. We should all be creeping around at night, stealing the enemy's weapons and putting sand in the oil pans of their Land Cruisers."

Uncle Abdel frowns as he considers this. "Perhaps you're right," he says at last. "Perhaps God is waiting for us to take some risks."

"Don't encourage her, brother!" Baba arrives, waggling his finger like an old woman. "You know as well as I do that children who sneak out of their homes at night get devoured by the Great Djinni Al Farouk."

"There are no children in this house," replies Abdel drily.

Baba and Uncle Abdel go into the house to talk, and stay

95

there until the four o'clock prayer call. When they reappear, they both look strained and anxious. They shake hands under the porch, clasping each other's elbows like members of some secret society.

"Good-bye, Kadi," calls Uncle Abdel, waving. "Be careful with that perfume of yours."

"I will, Uncle. Good-bye!"

As Uncle Abdel disappears into the rosy afternoon, Baba turns, looks left and right, then grasps my shoulders. "Can you keep a secret?" he asks.

He looks so serious and conspiratorial, I have a crazy urge to laugh.

"Yes," I squeak.

"Your uncle is worried about the security of the Ahmad Baba Library," he hisses. "You know, after what happened there the other day. He says we need to move the manuscripts to a safer location."

"Where can we move them to, Baba?"

"To our vault," he whispers.

☾

The hour before dusk in Timbuktu is always magical. Mud-brick buildings glow rose-red and the sweltering heat is relieved by a hint of a breeze.

A town crier is pacing the streets, summoning all of Timbuktu to Independence Square. The new regime is in need of a crowd immediately.

We dare not stay away. We gather six deep round the edges of the square, men and women on separate sides. All the women and girls are veiled. We exchange cautious greetings, identifying neighbors and friends from voices, hands, and feet.

Spotting Aisha's diamanté veil and Coca-Cola flip-flops, I

hurry toward her through the crowd. We embrace and I kiss her veiled cheek.

"Sorry about my voicemail," I tell her.

"It was priceless," she smiles. "Cheered me up."

We are interrupted by the arrival of the Defenders' Land Cruiser, with the black standard streaming behind it. Ten armed and turbaned boys are perching on the back, and Ali is one of them. I recognize him by his swollen eye.

Redbeard and Muhammad Zaarib get out of the cab and wave briefly at the crowd. Redbeard carries a megaphone and Zaarib a camel-hide whip. The townspeople stir uneasily. "*Hasbi rabijal Allah*," I whisper. Our defense is in God.

"Timbuktu is built on Islam," announces Redbeard, "and only Islamic law applies in it. Bring out the evildoers!"

The doors of the police station fly open and two veiled women are led out.

"Halimatu Tal," calls Redbeard. "Sitting in the marketplace without a veil. Twenty lashes."

"No!" I gasp.

It's Mama's friend, the millet pancake lady, the one who gives us free pancakes every time we pass.

Halimatu kneels down, shivering. Zaarib walks forward and stands behind his prisoner, his mouth a thin, hard line.

"*Ya Rabbu rham*," I murmur. Lord, have mercy.

Aisha grabs my hand and squeezes it.

The first harsh crack of the camel-hide whip resounds around the square. The kneeling woman gasps and flinches.

I screw my eyes shut under my veil and lose myself to *dhikr*. *Ya Rabbu rham. Ya Rabbu rham. Ya Rabbu rham.*

On the count of twenty I open my eyes. Halimatu has keeled over sideways and lies sobbing in the dust, her rib cage heaving.

I'm glad that's not me, I think, and straightaway I feel ashamed.

"Ramata ag Ahmed," announces Redbeard. "Walking in the marketplace with a transparent veil."

I know Ramata too. She was one of Tondi's bridesmaids the other night—a dark-skinned beauty, whirling in the moonlight. I remember the orange dress she wore, and the elegant cream sash.

She is not whirling now. She is crouching down on the balls of her feet, as if she's getting ready to milk a goat.

One. Two. Three. The whip flies to and fro, but Ramata makes no sound. She reaches down and scoops up a palmful of sand from the ground.

Four. Five. Six. Ramata's knuckles whiten round the sand. By the tenth lash, her whole arm is trembling.

The sand idea is common in Timbuktu. When a girl gives birth for the first time, her mother gives her a handful of sand to squeeze. *As soon as the sand turns to oil, my dear, then you can cry out loud.*

It never does, of course.

The cruel whip cuts Ramata's veil into ribbons across her back, but she stays silent until it's over. Unless she feels the slick sand-oil running over her fingertips, she will not even whimper.

A murmur of appreciation runs through the crowd.

"Good girl," whispers Aisha.

I couldn't do what Ramata is doing. I can't cope with pain at all. Soft and sweet, that's what Mama calls me. Soft and sweet like fresh-baked bread.

Eighteen . . . nineteen . . . twenty.

Zaarib scowls and raises his whip. He wants to carry on beating her until she cracks, but a word from Redbeard stops him.

"Next," says Redbeard. "Ali Konana. Playing unholy music in public. Twenty lashes."

No. He can't be serious.

Ali hops down from the trailer and strolls across the square to kneel before Zaarib. He folds his arms across his chest and waits for the whip. There are murmurs of surprise and nervous laughter from the assembled crowd. Are the Defenders really going to punish one of their own?

The first crack of the lash makes me jump.

"It's not his fault!" I want to yell. "I changed his ringtone as a joke!"

I stay silent, of course. I like the skin on my back. It keeps my insides safe.

Ali remains quiet for the first twelve lashes, but on the thirteenth he emits a long, drawn-out moo like a distraught cow.

Blindly I push my way back through the crowd, away from the truck and the whip and the pain. I can't bear it. I lift up my veil and bend low over a gutter, gulping great mouthfuls of air. I really can't bear it.

Manuscript 6,749: the tarikh of Sidi el Beckaye

Toward the end of the fifteenth century, there was a drought in Timbuktu. The rain did not fall. The wells became dry. All of the seventy-thousand people living in Timbuktu were in grave danger, and their animals as well.

The chief of Timbuktu called a meeting of the city elders to ask for their advice.

"There is a holy man called Sidi el Beckaye," said one of the elders, "who fasts all day and prays all night. Maybe he will help us."

"I will send the women and the children," said the chief, "and that will arouse his pity."

So the women and children of Timbuktu went to the house of Sidi el Beckaye, near the west gate of Timbuktu. They pleaded with him to pray to God for rain. "If we don't drink today, we will die," they told him.

Sidi el Beckaye was deeply moved. He burst out of his house and ran through the crowd like the Harmattan wind. He ran all the way out to the desert, west of the city, and there he lifted his foot and stamped with the strength of God. The desert shook from shore to shore, and all of Mali felt the tremors.

That single stomp from Sidi el Beckaye produced a foot-shaped well, and from the desert's adamantine bowels, fresh water bubbled up.

The well was named Sababou, Well of Destiny, and still today it waters Timbuktu.

Sidi el Beckaye, that hot-headed saint who ran and stamped, was given the name Tamba-Tamba, which means Fast-Fast. Every Friday evening, people gather at his shrine, to thank him for the water he provides.

Ali

Shirtless, I recline beside the shrine of Tamba-Tamba, watching videos on my phone, alone. Even lying on my front like this, my back still stings. If anything, it's getting worse.

Aside from the physical pain, there is the question which has bothered me all afternoon. *Why didn't I simply tell Redbeard that Kadi changed my ringtone?*

"Peace be upon you, Loppa-Loppa!" calls Jabir. He and Omar are heading my way through the deepening dusk. Jabir holds a can of paint and a blackened brush. Omar's water bottle is slung over his shoulder, and he carries a large glass jar of something dark.

I stop the video. "Peace be upon you too," I say. "Where have you been?"

"Censoring," says Jabir. "Blotting out pictures on billboards and walls. Men, women, cows, that sort of thing. Pictures are against God's law."

"You missed my punishment."

"We heard about it," says Omar. "We brought you some honey."

My back hurts so much I can hardly think straight, and it takes me a second or two to remember what honey is. "Thanks," I say. "I'm not hungry."

"It's not for eating," says Omar. "It will reduce the swelling and stop your stripes getting infected."

Omar hangs his water bottle on one of the rodier-palm bundles that protrude from the wall of Tamba-Tamba's shrine. He kneels down beside me and opens the glass jar. My lash wounds prickle and smart as he drizzles the honey across my back.

"Al-Nahl verse sixty-nine," whispers Omar. "*There issues from the body of the bee a liquid of varying colors, wherein is healing for mankind.*"

There are tears in my eyes, but not of pain. "Thank you, Omar. I don't know what I'd do without you."

Jabir picks up my phone. "What were you watching?" he asks.

Before I can stop him, he presses Play.

"Give me that!" I reach across to grab the phone, but I'm too late. The video is playing.

"*Two hundred francs? We could get a bag of* real *white men's ears for that!*"

"Nice!" whoops Jabir. "Who are they?"

"It's those girls from La Détente," says Omar, craning his neck to look. "Why were you filming them, Ali?"

"Because they're troublemakers."

Jabir whistles. "They certainly are," he says. "Hey, you should show this to Zaarib. They'll get twenty lashes for walking in the marketplace unveiled."

"I filmed it ages ago," I lie. "These days they both wear veils."

Jabir returns the video to the beginning and presses Play

again. "Veils were first ordained because of girls like that," he says. "Makes you crazy, doesn't it?"

"*Avert your gaze from all forbidden things*," quotes Omar. "Perhaps we should not be watching."

"Of course we should," says Jabir. "We need to recognize the troublemakers."

"Really?" Omar gets to his feet. "And how will you recognize them, now that they're wearing veils?"

"By their voices," says Jabir. "I will make them repeat the phrase *white men's ears* three times."

"Come on, you idiot. It's time for sunset prayers."

Omar and Jabir go off to find their prayer mats, leaving me alone.

How will I recognize her if she is wearing a veil?

I will recognize her jaunty walk, I will recognize her oleander scent, and I will recognize her bubbling, high-pitched laugh, which is like the chirp of a bronze-winged mannikin.

Of course, I don't want Kadija lashed. If you lash a girl like that, you lose her forever. This way she has a second chance. By having mercy on her, I have proved to her the rightness of our cause.

I have purchased her soul for God.

☾

The sunset prayer call is blaring from the many minarets of Timbuktu.

God is patient with the sick. He who cannot stand to pray may sit, and he who cannot sit may lie. The important thing is to commune with God.

I wash my hands and close my eyes, force Kadija from my mind, and start to say my prayers. Halfway through Al-Fatiha, I am interrupted by the voice of an old woman.

"Tamba-Tamba, we beseech you!
Cows must drink and sheep must wash,
The little donkeys must quench their thirst.
Tamba-Tamba, send the rain!"

By Tamba-Tamba's tomb she stands, veiled in black, and chanting witlessly.

I lift my head. "Who let you in?" I ask.

"Do not fear," croaks the woman.

"I'm not afraid, I'm repulsed. Who let you in here?"

The old woman cups a hand over her ear. "What's that you say?"

"Who let you in?"

"The sentry."

"And who are you praying to?"

"Tamba-Tamba."

"Stop," I tell her straight. "The crock of bones inside this tomb is even deafer than you, old crone, and blind and mute as well."

"What's that you say?"

"Pray to God!" I shout. "No one else. And if it's water you want, my friend's water bottle is hanging on one of those rodier branches right in front of you."

She turns and shuffles off. I must tell Redbeard that some of our sentries are letting people into the camp to pray to Tamba-Tamba. It's not just idolatry, it's a security breach as well.

☾

At nine o'clock my phone rings. Not that stupid rap song—I deleted that—but a harmless, natural ringtone, the whirr of insect legs.

It's Kadija.

"*Foofo*," she whispers. "How's your back?"

"Fine. We should not be talking."

"I'll keep it short. I just wanted to tell you"—she hesitates, then seems to change her mind—"I can't believe they lashed one of their own."

"I insisted," I say.

"*You insisted?*"

"All right, a boy called Hamza insisted. But he was correct. Sharia applies as much to us as it does to you."

She tuts. "Baba says you don't care about Islam. He says this whole thing is about money and power."

"He's wrong, Kadija. People call us terrorists and monsters because they dare not believe that we are acting out of love. We advocate sharia because sharia keeps society healthy. It is a blessing on us all."

"I see. And is your back feeling blessed tonight?"

"My friend just put some honey on it. *There issues from the body of the bee a liquid of varying colors, wherein is healing for mankind. There is certainly a sign in that for people who reflect.*"

Kadi yawns loudly. "You wear me out with all your words, Ali. You think your studies make you wise, but you're wrong. There's more of God in one glance from Imam Karim than there is in all your talk." She pauses, and then blurts out what she has been leading up to all this time, her big confession.

"You do know it was me who changed your ringtone, don't you?"

"Of course."

"You're not angry?"

"Not anymore," I say. "Were you watching when it rang?"

"Yes," she says. "I was hoping that your Arab master might leap to his feet and do the Loppa-Loppa dance."

"Have some respect!"

"Sorry."

105

Her apology takes me by surprise. Perhaps I'm getting through to her at last.

"Ali," she whispers. "Is someone replacing you on patrol tonight? It's just that I'm scared of looters. If no one is patrolling, what's to stop them breaking into our house and—"

"Trust in God," I tell her. "God is replacing me on patrol tonight."

"All right," she whispers. "Pass the night in peace."

☾

Omar unrolls his mat and lies down next to me.

"I need your advice," I tell him, "and don't say there are two schools of thought, or I'll break your nose. Is it wrong for a boy and a girl to talk on the telephone?"

Omar whistles through his teeth and begins to recite in Arabic. "Al-Ahzab thirty-two," he says. "*Be not soft in speech, lest diseased hearts should be moved with desire.*"

"What does that mean?"

"It means phone her if you need to, but don't talk about soft things."

"Soft things?"

"Feelings. Desires. Needs."

"Can we talk about books?"

"You can talk about the Holy Book," says Omar. "The Book is not a soft thing. But other books are mostly soft."

We lie in silence for a long time. I turn my head and watch my namesake rising in the east, imparting strength to my torn, bruised body. The stars and the honey will work God's will. Tomorrow, *inshallah*, I shall be well.

"One more thing," says Omar, jolting me awake. "If a boy is thinking about proposing marriage to a girl, he is allowed to look at her unveiled, to help him decide, I mean."

"Are you sure?"

"When Jabir ibn Abdullah, peace be upon him, was considering marriage, he hid in the girl's garden every evening for a week to catch a glimpse of her."

"I don't know why you're telling me this. It's not like I'm considering marriage."

"I know you're not. I'm just saying."

༄

"Ali!"

I jolt to instant wakefulness. My hand flies to my knife.

"What is it?" I cry. "Omar, is that you?"

I lift myself up on one elbow and light my paraffin lamp. As the flame flickers into life, Omar's face looms in front of me, yellow and bloated. He is wheezing painfully, trying to speak again. His frightened eyes stare horribly from their sockets.

"Omar!" I cry. "My God, what's happening to you?"

He tilts his head back and his mouth gapes open. His tongue is blocking his airway, huge and purple like an eggplant. He can't breathe.

"Help!" I shout. "Master! Anyone! Come and help!"

I push Omar down onto his side, hook my finger into his mouth, and pull the tongue clear of the airway. But still he cannot breathe because his throat is swollen too.

"Master!" I yell.

I put my hand on Omar's heart. The blood is slow and weak.

"Omar, stay with me," I plead. "Whatever you do, don't die. Redbeard is coming, Omar. He'll know what's wrong with you. He'll know what to do."

Kadija

My father opens his eyes and sits bolt upright before I even say a word.

"Kadi, what's wrong?"

"There is no one patrolling our street," I tell him. "I've been watching for a whole hour, and there's nobody at all."

"Good girl." Baba reaches for his plastic kettle and splashes water on his face. "You told your uncle that you wanted to do some creeping around at night. Well, now's your chance."

"What's going on?" mumbles Mama, half asleep.

"Unlock the vault," Baba tells her, "and light the lamps."

"What about me?" I ask. "What shall I do?"

He takes a notebook from under his pillow and thrusts it into my hands. "Take that," he says. "There are three telephone numbers on the back page. Call them."

"And say what?"

"Say it's time to gather the horsemen of the sun."

Baba puts on his turban and a long white robe. He hurries to and fro with bit and bridle, stirrups and saddle. I ring the numbers one by one, conveying the cryptic message.

"Who needs the radio when we've got the Timbuktu Telegraph?" grins Baba, yanking tight Marimba's stomach strap and fastening the buckles.

"Each of those three people will phone three other people—and each of those in turn will phone three people. That makes forty heads of family with an average of twelve people in their compounds."

Genius. In five minutes flat we have five hundred men, women, and children all around the city, dressed and ready for action.

☾

Pucci naange, horsemen of the sun, are big, orange ants. In hot season you see long columns of them out in the bush, carrying their treasures on their shoulders. That's exactly what we are going to do tonight.

Five hundred volunteers are lined up outside the Ahmad Baba Library. It is rare to see a queue in Timbuktu, but tonight my father has insisted on it. "Tonight, we are an army," he says. "We must be orderly, and fast."

Aisha and I stand arm in arm, awaiting our turn. When we arrive at the front of the queue, Uncle Abdel thanks us solemnly and hands us dark blue treasure trunks. We raise the trunks onto our braided heads and traipse the length of Askia Street.

The lofty Djinguereber Mosque regards us as we pass. Baba regards us too. Up and down he rides on his white stallion, supervising the horsemen of the sun. There are twenty manuscripts inside each trunk, many of them priceless.

To tell the truth, I'm worried for Baba. Looking after two

thousand manuscripts during this occupation has made him stressed and jittery. How will he cope with twelve thousand?

"Look, no hands," whispers Aisha, as soon as my father is out of sight.

"Stop that. Hold it properly," I hiss. I too am feeling the strain.

"I've got an idea," she says. "Let's take our boxes down the road to the port at Kabara, rent a canoe, and travel upriver to Bamako. We can sell the manuscripts to a collector and use the profits to visit Switzerland. Think of all the chocolate we could buy."

Aisha is always going on about Swiss chocolate, ever since we read that "Taste of Paradise" article in my *Jeune Afrique* magazine. Neither of us has tasted chocolate, of course, and probably never will.

"Don't even joke about selling the manuscripts," I tell her.

"Listen to yourself," she mutters. "Anyone would think you were a Guardian already."

We turn into our courtyard and stack the trunks in the open air.

"I don't understand," says Aisha. "How is this more secure than the library?"

"Baba knows what he's doing."

Only seven people know about our secret vault: Baba, Mama, me, Uncle Abdel, Aunt Juma, Cousin Yusuf, and his little sister, Kamisa. We have to keep it that way. As soon as the horsemen of the sun have gone, the real work begins.

We form a chain to move the five hundred trunks down to the vault. Baba and Abdel are above ground. Yusuf and Aunt Juma are on the steps. Mama, Kamisa, and I are in the vault itself. Mama is wearing her organizing face and her prattle is constant and reassuring. "Come on, carefully does it, let me help you. Well done, girls."

My cousin Kamisa is only eleven, poor thing. Her eyes are big and tired, and the weight of the trunks makes her stagger, but she is determined to work as hard as the rest of us.

"Kamisa, take a rest," says Mama. "If you continue like this, your arms will drop off."

"I'm fine," Kamisa groans. "This is the most fun I've had in ages."

Mama frowns. She is trying to work out whether her niece is being sarcastic.

By the time the call to prayer rings out over Timbuktu, the vault is packed from floor to ceiling, with only a narrow aisle down the middle. I walk along the aisle and the dark blue trunks tower above me on either side like walls of standing water. I imagine I am the Prophet Musa parting the Sea of Reeds, leading God's people from slavery to freedom. How does it go again? *So We revealed to Musa, "Strike the sea with your staff." And it split in two, each part like a towering cliff.*

Our family's manuscript collection has grown sixfold in one night. The thought of all those manuscripts makes me giddy with pleasure, and Baba giddy with anxiety.

I go to see Tondi at first light. She has run away from her husband and is back in her parents' house. I am not worried for her. It is traditional for a new bride to run away a few times in the first month. It stops her being taken for granted.

I arrive to find her milking a black-and-white cow. Its calf has a rope round its neck, which Tondi holds fast between her teeth.

She takes the rope out of her mouth to greet me. "Hello, Kadi. You look terrible."

"Not much sleep," I say. "How's marriage?"

"Not much sleep," she says with a grin. "I wish I didn't have to keep escaping." She puts the rope back in her mouth and carries on milking the cow. The calf can smell the milk and is straining to get closer.

"That thing is going to pull your teeth out," I tell her, taking off my veil. "Here, let me help you."

Tondi holds the calf tight and I crouch down in her place. I put the wooden pail beneath my knees, then carefully palm the teats and start to squeeze. The first squirt lubricates my hands, the rest is for the pail.

"Have you heard the news?" says Tondi. "Tamba-Tamba has returned to save us."

Her dark eyes shine as she tells the story. At sunrise she was carrying a pail of milk past the military camp and found the Defenders in disarray. The sentry told her that one of the boys died in the night, right next to the shrine of Tamba-Tamba.

My hand slips on the teat, causing the startled cow to flick me with its tail, right in my eyes.

"Which one?" I ask, trying to sound casual. "Which boy is dead?"

"No idea," says Tondi. "They all look the same to me. Black shirts, black turbans, beautiful teeth. Where are you going, Kadi? There's still milk in that udder!"

I fling my veil back on and hurry away from Tondi and the cows.

It's him, I think, breaking into a run. It's him and he's died of his injuries and it's all my fault.

I head toward the military camp with phone in hand, squinting through tears as I scroll through the *A*s.

Adama, Ahadu, Ahmed, Aisha, *Ali*.

His phone rings for an age, and then, praise be to God, he answers. "Yes?"

"Is that you, Ali?"

"Yes."

"I heard there was a death in the camp. I was afraid it might be you."

"I wish it had been." Ali's voice is brittle and he sounds younger somehow. "It was my best friend."

"I'm sorry," I say. "What was his name?"

"Omar." His voice trembles, then cracks. "He wasn't even sick!"

"I'm sorry," I repeat. "Ali, where are you?"

"The other boys are out of their minds with fear. They're saying Saint Tamba-Tamba killed him."

"Where are you, Ali?"

A long silence, then finally he answers. "Same place as always. On the tire outside your house."

❮

Sure enough there he is, sitting on his tire in the early-morning sun.

I cross the street and whisper a greeting. "Peace be upon you, Ali. How's your back?"

"Fine," he says, not looking up. He is writing with a quill on an oblong board.

"You don't usually patrol during the day," I say.

"I missed last night. I must make up the hours."

Looking at his board upside down, I recognize Al-Fatiha, the opening verses of the Qur'an.

> "In the name of God, the Compassionate and Merciful.
> Praise be to God, Lord of all the worlds.
> The Compassionate, the Merciful, Ruler on the Day of
>   Reckoning.
> You alone do we worship, and You alone do we ask for help.
> Guide us on the straight path,

113

The path of those who have received your grace;
Not the path of those who have incurred wrath, nor of
those who wander astray.
Amen."

"Have you buried your friend?" I say.

"Yes."

"May he drink the water of Paradise."

Ali is supposed to say "Amen" to that, but he doesn't. He scowls up at me with sudden hatred in his eyes.

"You know who killed him, don't you?"

"No," I say. "I don't know anything. You said that Tamba-Tamba—"

"Rubbish. That's what the other boys are saying, but they're wrong, aren't they? Omar was murdered by one of your people masquerading as an old woman."

He's mad, poor boy. His grief has sent him mad.

Ali babbles on, his fingers tense like claws against his writing board. "It's easy to don a black veil and to fake a croaky voice, isn't it? Easy to talk your way past a sentry and slip something evil into a water bottle hanging on the wall. Which one of you was it, Kadi? That drummer with the long hair? Or that other boy, the one who's not your boyfriend? Oh, your veils make fine disguises, don't they? I'll bet you've all been having a good laugh about it."

I reach out and lay a hand on Ali's shoulder. He shakes it off.

"The water bottle was hanging on the shrine right next to me. Was it me you meant to kill?"

"No!"

He takes a ragged breath, then frowns. "Oleander," he whispers. "Of course."

"What?"

114

"It was you, wasn't it, Kadi? You put oleander in Omar's water bottle!"

"No!" I back away. "Don't be stupid!"

"It was!" His hand shoots out and grabs my ankle. "It was you, and I'm going to prove it!"

He pulls my flip-flop off my left foot, throws down his writing board, and hobbles away toward the military camp, out of his mind with grief.

I sit on the tire and wait for him. There's nothing else to do. I imagine him crawling around the shrine of Tamba-Tamba with his nose to the ground, searching for a flip-flop print that matches mine. It would be funny if it weren't so sad.

A key scrapes in a lock. Our heavy front door creaks. Mama and Baba emerge from the archway and step out blinking into the light.

"Kadi!" exclaims my mother. "We thought you were still sleeping. How did you get out?"

"I didn't want to wake you," I tell them, nodding toward the sycamore tree in front of our house.

They look up at the balustrade and the slender upper branches of the tree.

"Sorry," I say, before they can tell me off.

"Don't do it again," says Baba. "Listen, Kadi, I'm going to the town hall and your mother is going to the market. Why don't you go along with her?"

"I can't. I'm waiting for my flip-flop." Even to my own ears this sounds an odd excuse, so I add, "It's being mended."

My parents accept this without question. I guess they have a lot else on their minds. Baba strides off up the street, and Mama follows at a safe distance. It's crazy, but even husbands and wives have been warned against walking together in public.

I sit on the tire and wait for Ali to return.

Here he comes, poor creature, hobbling painfully. He comes right up close without a word, then kneels down in front of me and tries to slip my flip-flop on.

His fingers brush against the side of my foot.

I'm sure he didn't mean to touch me, but all the same, girls have been lashed for less. I bend forward clumsily, and he stands up just at the wrong time. The top of his head hits me in the mouth.

"Sorry," he mumbles.

I raise the back of my hand to my mouth. My lip is bleeding, but not badly.

"Find anything?" I ask.

He clenches his jaw and nods. I wait for him.

"A scorpion," he says at last. "One of those stupid see-through ones, lying there squashed on Omar's sleeping mat. I didn't see it before. Redbeard reckons that's what killed him."

"No way," I say. "A scorpion sting can't kill you."

"It can if you're allergic, Redbeard says. If you're allergic, your throat swells up, and your blood slows down, and you die." He picks up his wooden writing board and clasps it in both hands.

"I see. So you don't think he was poisoned?"

"No." He looks away and scowls. "But it makes no difference. Even if he wasn't killed by the enemy, he was still here on a mission from God, so that makes him a martyr, doesn't it? He got what he always wanted, didn't he?"

"I don't know."

Ali switches suddenly to Arabic. "*Paradise has been decorated for him,*" he chants, "*and beautiful women are calling upon him— 'Come, oh commander with the order of God'—and they are dressed in their best attire.*"

This is awkward. I cast round and say the first thing that comes into my head.

"I like your handwriting, Ali."

He blinks and looks down at his writing board as if seeing it for the first time. "Al-Fatiha," he murmurs. "When I was three, I could recite it. When I was five, I could write it by myself. At seven I sensed its beauty, and by the time I turned nine, there were only two things in the world that thrilled me to the spleen: playing soccer and reading Al-Fatiha. It's only seven verses, yet the whole Book lies within."

"*If I spoke to you of Al-Fatiha,*" I quote softly, "*my words would overburden seventy camels.*"

"Who said that?"

"I can't remember."

"Omar would know," says Ali. "He had a memory like a sheikh, that man. An answer for everything—" He breaks off.

I know it's dangerous to start feeling sorry for this boy, but I can't help it. He should be at home in Goundam right now, or walking tall behind a herd of cows, not squatting on a tire in Timbuktu, confused and miserable.

I glance at my phone. It is nearly nine o'clock. Baba is at the town hall with the elders and Mama is at the market.

Aisha wants to slit Ali's throat with a kora string, but I don't. I want to cheer him up and then, if such a thing is possible, to rescue him.

"Would you like to see something beautiful?" I ask.

☾

I run into our yard, and down into the vault. The manuscript locations log book is on the table at the foot of the steps. I flick through it until I find what I am looking for: "Illuminated Al-Fatiha, Trunk Twelve."

I open the lid of trunk twelve and delve inside. The illuminated manuscript smiles up at me, gorgeous as always.

Clasping the precious Al-Fatiha under my veil, I run up the stairs, past the horse, out into the street, and smack into my father, who is back from the town hall. The topmost folio of the manuscript slips from under my veil and drops to the sand.

"What have you got there?" says Baba.

"Nothing."

He bends to pick up the folio. His eyes, which looked so tired a moment ago, ignite with rage.

"How dare you!" he stutters, grabbing my elbow. "Come inside this minute!"

"Baba, please don't be angry—"

"Kadija, how many times have I told you never to take manuscripts outside this house, yet you deliberately disobey me!"

He marches me into the yard, snaps a supple branch off the neem tree, and strips it of its leaves.

"I'm sorry, Baba."

"So am I," he says, raising the branch.

I turn my back and brace myself for the blow. Baba hasn't beaten me since I was five years old, and that was also to do with the manuscripts. I was playing with our one and only key to the ancient door of the vault, and somehow I mislaid it. I remember Baba's exact words: *Perhaps a neem tree branch will jog your memory.* As it turned out, he was right.

Still the blow has not landed. I hear an apologetic cough, and turn to look. Ali has come in through the entrance archway. He is standing there, holding a sheep on a short rope.

"What do you want?" snaps Baba, lowering the neem branch.

"I brought your ewe back," says Ali. "I found her wandering in the street."

"I don't keep sheep," scowls Baba. "That animal belongs to my brother Abdel next door."

"Right. I see." Ali shuffles his feet and stares at the ground, but does not leave.

"What now?" says Baba.

"It's none of my business," says Ali, "but neem branches do not make good canes. That camel-hide whip they used on me yesterday—it stings like the fire of hell, I promise you. The end is split into three strands, you see, and the strands are hardened with salt. Perhaps we could lend it to you for a little while."

"Get out of my sight," says Baba.

Ali puts his hand across his heart, a gesture of respect, and strolls out into the street, leading Uncle Abdel's sheep behind him.

"He's a brute," says Baba, scowling.

"Yes."

Baba looks down at the neem branch in his hand. An awkward silence passes between us. Then he throws the branch on the ground and stomps off to the vault to replace his precious manuscript.

☾

That night, once more, I drag my sleeping mat to the edge of the roof, beside the balustrade. I put my paraffin lamp on the mat and turn its orange flame down low.

Ali is sitting on his tire, whittling a piece of wood. I fasten my veil with a silver pin and find his number in my phone.

Climb the tree I text in French.

No

I'm veiled

Still no

I have something to show you

What?

An illuminated Al-Fatiha

OK

Ali walks to the tree, glances up and down the deserted street, and starts to climb. He swings himself up into the heart of the tree and makes his way along a branch, pedaling the air. With both hands he grasps the balustrade and hangs there, gathering his strength. Then, with a final effort, he swings himself up and over.

"*Foofo*," he says, wincing in pain. Hi.

"*Foofo*."

He looks at me and frowns. "That's not the veil I gave you."

"I'll wear your veil another time. What were you working on down there?"

"This." He holds out a rice spoon. "You can have it if you like. It's sandalwood."

I take the spoon and turn it over in my hands. The handle is tapered and slightly curved. The head is beautifully smooth. I touch my heart in gratitude.

"I'm only here to talk about the Book," he says. "The Book is not soft."

"What do you mean, not soft?"

"Forget it."

He sits down on the edge of my mat and I pass him a beaker of water. He takes a sip and uses the rest to wash his hands, wrists, and forearms.

I pick up the manuscript by the edges and place it in front of him. "Be careful," I whisper. "It's almost three hundred years old."

"Wow." He traces a finger over the ornate letters, the calligraphic swirls, the radiant blue ink. "Hausawi script," he says. "From Nigeria, right?"

"That's right," I say, delighted. "A truly African Al-Fatiha."

"It's magnificent."

I lean back on my hands and close my eyes as he recites the sacred verses under his breath. He reads them through three times, then trails off into satisfied silence.

"I adore Arabic," I murmur. "They say that reading the Book in any other language is like being kissed through a veil."

"Really?"

"Yes." My cheeks feel suddenly hot. "I mean, yes, they really say it. I wouldn't know whether they are right, those people."

"Do you have more?"

"More what?"

"More manuscripts."

"No."

He cocks his head on one side. Does he know I'm lying?

I change the subject clumsily. "Thank you for saving me today, Ali. Bringing my uncle's sheep and offering to lend him a whip. Ha! He was so angry at you that he forgot to be angry at me. Except that now he thinks you're a stupid thug."

Ali makes a little click deep down in his throat. "And what do you think?"

"I think you're a clever thug."

The faintest trace of a smile plays around the corner of his mouth. For the first time ever, I am grateful for the veil that protects me from his scrutiny.

Pull yourself together, I tell myself.

Ali leans toward me, and for one crazy moment I think he's going to kiss me through my veil. Not that I want him to, of course. He's the invader. The oppressor. An enemy of Timbuktu.

"Kadi," he whispers. "It's *haram*. Forbidden."

"What is?"

"Perfume."

"In God's name!" I cry. "Are you incapable of having a conversation without using the word *haram*?"

To my horror, Baba's voice rises from the courtyard below. "Kadi, who are you talking to up there?"

"Baba, please, I'm on the phone!" I shout.

Ali frowns. "You shouldn't lie to your father."

"All right," I say. "I'll tell him you're here." I lift the veil to uncover the lower half of my face, and open my mouth as if to shout.

I've got no intention of actually shouting. It's just a joke, as any normal person would realize. But Ali's eyes widen in fear, and he lurches at me with his fingers outstretched to smother my shout.

I giggle and dodge to one side, thrusting out a hand to steady myself. A stupid, clumsy, sacrilegious hand.

What have I done? God, what have I done?

Ali didn't see where my hand came down. He didn't hear the quiet sickening crunch, the unmistakable brittle snap of ancient paper fibers. He has no idea of the damage he has done. His hand is over my mouth, and he's grinning like a minstrel on a feast day.

Grinning!

Why is he even here, this dolt? Why did I invite him up to this most intimate of all places? To impress him? To convert him? To seek forgiveness for the lash scars on his back?

I knock his hand away and hiss, "Get off my roof this minute."

He leans back, smiling. He thinks I'm joking.

I snatch my veil, rip it off, and stare my enemy full in the face. "You heard me, Ali. Get off this roof!"

For a moment I think he is going to refuse, but I keep on staring until he averts his eyes. In one sudden catlike movement he vaults the balustrade, grabs a branch and swings down out of sight, and only when he's gone do I dare look down to inspect the damage.

Yes, it's bad. A large fragment has flaked off the corner of the holy folio.

God curse me. God smite me with leprosy. God make every one of my stupid clumsy fingers wither and drop off! In spite of all my training, the countless hours I've spent with manuscripts, I have broken the oldest African Al-Fatiha in the world.

I look up at the stars, wheeling and spinning in their orbits. The stars don't care. Why should they?

There is nothing for it but to destroy the evidence. I pick up the flake of paper and put it in my mouth, pressing it hard against my palate until it has completely dissolved.

I wince.

I did not expect such sweet words to taste so bitter.

☽

In the morning, two truckloads of light-skinned fighters arrive. They are speaking Arabic in loud, uncultured voices and they have rocket launchers on the backs of their trucks instead of machine guns.

Sitting on my roof, I watch Redbeard come out of the military camp to greet the newcomers. He embraces them like old friends, his leathery face cracking into a series of tangled smiles.

I jump up and hurry down the tree trunk two notches at a time. "Mama," I say. "More fighters have arrived."

Mama is not alone. Aunt Juma is with her. Both of them have long faces.

"What's wrong?" I ask. "What's happened?"

"It's your cousin, Kamisa," says Mama. "She's been arrested in the marketplace for not wearing a veil. They say they are going to flog her in the square next week."

"Kamisa is only eleven! They can't arrest an eleven-year-old girl."

"She only went to buy onions." Aunt Juma wrings her hands. "She was wearing her veil when she went out. She must have gotten hot and taken it off."

"Does Baba know?"

"Yes," says Mama. "He is going to speak with the elders this afternoon."

"A posse of jabbering old men. What can they do?"

I brace myself for a storm of disapproval, but none comes. Mama and Aunt Juma know as well as I do that the men of Timbuktu have done what they can to save our city, and sadly they have failed.

It's time for the women of Timbuktu to act.

☾

The phone network in Timbuktu is terrible these days. It takes me half an hour to get a signal, and seven tries before my call goes through. When finally Ali answers, I don't say anything about last night. I just get straight to the point.

"Ali, they've arrested my cousin Kamisa for not wearing a veil. They're going to lash her in the square next week."

"I see." He pauses. "Is she strong?"

"Of course she's not strong! She's eleven! I want you to talk to Redbeard and persuade him to show mercy."

"We do not make the law," says Ali. "We simply follow it."

"Come on, Ali. What about Al-Fatiha? *In the name of God, the Compassionate and Merciful.* You read it last night. You recite it five times every day. Don't you think it's time to practice it? I'm asking you to talk to your master, that's all."

There is a long pause, and when Ali finally replies his voice sounds small and plaintive, like a little boy's.

"He would not listen even if I did."

"I thought we were friends, Ali!"

The line goes dead. Either he has hung up on me or the network is down again. Either way, I'm properly angry now. Angry with the regime for arresting Kamisa. Angry with Ali for making me plead. Angry with myself for being weak and showing it.

Timbuktu women are not weak. It's time we remembered that.

Aunt Juma and Mama are in the courtyard, pounding sumbala and cinnamon sticks.

"Auntie," I hear myself say, "where is Kamisa being held?"

"In a cell at the police station."

"Then we shall march on the police station," I tell them. "Just us women. Tomorrow, after Friday prayers."

They have stopped pounding now. They are staring at me like I've turned into a bearded djinni.

"Do you think they will take any notice?" says Aunt Juma.

"They will have to," I say. "We will march unveiled."

༄

Once again the Timbuktu Telegraph has worked its magic. Since yesterday morning, all the gossip in the marketplace and mosque has been about the women's protest march. We meet after Friday prayers, as planned, at the monument of Al Farouk.

We are getting good at recognizing our friends and neighbors by their veils. I spot Aisha's diamanté veil a mile off, and push through the crowd to get to her.

We embrace tightly.

"I hear all this was your idea." She grins. "Do you think it will help Kamisa?"

"I hope so, yes. But it's not just about Kamisa, is it? It's about every girl and woman in the city."

"You know you're crazy, don't you?"

"Sure. When did I last have an idea that wasn't crazy?"

Fatimata, the first wife of the mayor, has agreed to lead the protest. She steps up now onto the pedestal of Al Farouk, wearing a beautiful dark blue robe and matching veil. When she raises her hands for silence, her long sleeves drop down a little, revealing intricate henna tattoos on her wrists and forearms.

"Women of Timbuktu!" she cries. "There is nothing wrong with veils!"

That's not right. That's not what she's supposed to say.

"Veils are good," she declares, "and in the future of this great city we will always need them!"

I glance sideways at Aisha, who is shaking her head. Either the mayor's wife has lost her mind, or she has turned traitor. Money is a powerful persuader, particularly in these difficult times.

"We will always need veils," cries Fatimata, "for recently born babies, recently married brides, and recently dead corpses!"

A cheer goes up from the assembled girls and women. Aisha punches the air.

"For Tuareg men and for highwaymen!"

A ripple of laughter, and clapping.

"But not for young women in the street!"

Cheers of agreement.

"Or old women in the mosque!"

More cheers.

"Or eleven-year-old girls like Kamisa Diallo, buying onions in the marketplace!"

Aunt Juma is standing to one side of the pedestal wearing her lime green veil. Her fists are clenched, and at the mention of her daughter, her shoulders start shaking. Mama steps closer to her sister-in-law and curls an arm around her waist.

"This is not Riyadh," cries the mayor's wife. "This is not

Jeddah. This is not Islamabad. Sisters, this is Timbuktu, the city of three hundred and thirty-three saints!"

Aisha throws back her head and trills her tongue at the back of her throat so loud that I have to clap my hands over my ears. The ululation catches on. It sweeps through the crowd from one impassioned tongue to the next. It echoes from the stern facades of the town hall, the police station, and the Sidi Yahya Mosque, more potent and formidable than any war cry.

Fatimata puts her hands over her eyes as if in prayer. "Timbuktu is Muslim," she shouts, "but the women of Timbuktu do not walk veiled!"

With that, she removes the veil that hides her eyes and throws it in the air. The black fabric billows, curls, and drops silently into the dust. Fatimata stands there on the pedestal with her painted eyebrows, tattooed lips and double chin on full display, glaring round as if daring us to even think the word *haram*.

Aunt Juma takes off her lime green veil, rips it down the middle, and drops the two halves at her feet. Mama does the same with hers.

Aisha lets go of my hand. "This is it," she says. "No going back." She slowly lifts her diamanté veil to reveal her long neck, gleaming teeth, and thick unbraided hair. She steps on a corner of the veil and yanks it with both hands. The fabric stretches, then ladders, and with a coarse rasping sound it tears in two.

I told Ali I would wear his gift someday, and I have been as good as my word. I wish he were here for this moment. I push a fold of the veil between my teeth, bite a small hole in the cheap fabric, and hook one finger from each hand into the hole. With one hard pull, the veil splits and the unforgiving Mali sun bursts in on me.

Moments such as this gave Independence Square its name. The women of Timbuktu are laughing, cheering, and clawing at their veils. Dust rises around the Al Farouk monument. Spontaneous dancing has broken out. A discarded veil lands on the statue itself, and for one glorious, sacrilegious moment the great Protector Djinni shares a jaunty scarlet headdress with his horse.

Blinking and squinting in the sun, we form ourselves into ranks and advance shoulder to shoulder toward the police station. Badji Dikko, the woman directly in front of me, is shaking both fists in the air as she walks.

Libérons Kamisa, Rejetons le voile!

Free Kamisa, reject the veil! Free Kamisa, reject the veil! The chant ebbs and swells on the shimmering air as we march toward the seat of the Defenders' power. For the first time since the invasion, they are their name and we are the Aggressors. The bare-faced women of Timbuktu are marching toward their destiny, unarmed, unveiled, and unstoppable.

My phone vibrates against my thigh. A text from Ali.

Run, Kadi. Run.

The doors of the police station fly open and two lines of Defenders jog out into the light. One line of black-clad boys turns left, the other line turns right. They spread out along the white-washed walls of Independence Square and raise their AK-47s to their shoulders.

The last man out the door is Redbeard himself. He stands on the top step of the police station and surveys the scene.

Comedy or menace? Which does he see when he looks at us?

"Armez!" calls Redbeard.

Ready! The boys' backs stiffen. Their eyes focus. Their hands tighten on their guns.

I see Ali before he sees me, on the far right of the line. Even from this distance I can see his knees are trembling.

He's afraid. Until this moment I have never seen him afraid.

We are still moving forward, but the mood has changed. Big Fatimata glances over her shoulder at the women and girls behind her. Is she looking to us for courage? We hardly have enough for ourselves. Are they bluffing, these boys, or have they been instructed to shoot us in cold blood?

"*Pointe!*"

Aim! There is some fidgeting along the line as each Defender lines up his sights. Badji Dikko stops abruptly, causing me to bump into her from behind.

"*Feu!*"

Gunfire and screaming fill my ears. Badji whirls round, eyes wide in craven fear, elbowing me in the face in her hurry to escape. Aisha and I fling ourselves to the ground, and then we are being trampled and kicked and the deafening rattle of automatic weapons is all around us and I just want it to stop.

☾

The two hospitals in Timbuktu are full. Girls and women cram the wards and spill out into the corridors. Crush injuries and broken bones are everywhere, but there is not a single gunshot wound. Redbeard's men were firing over our heads, and we did not realize it until we had panicked and trampled each other half to death.

That night I visit Aisha at the Kabara Road Hospital, where she is being treated for concussion. There are seven patients in the tiny room, and visitors too. It's chaos.

Mama Diabaté is sitting on a corner of Aisha's mat, with her daughter's diamanté veil in her hand. She is sewing the two halves neatly back together.

"Peace be upon you, Mama Diabaté."

"And upon you, *ma chérie*."

"How is Aisha?"

"She woke up about half an hour ago but went straight back to sleep again."

"Were you at the protest, Mama?"

"All six minutes of it." She smiles ruefully, then reaches over to press something into my palm. "Aisha said to give you this."

I look down at the kora string necklace in my hand, and the corners of my eyes prick with tears. I lift it over my head and arrange it on my throat.

"Thank you, Mama," I say.

It is not just manuscripts that suffer chipping. People do as well. All around the city, our friends' and neighbors' spirits are flaking away piece by piece. Soon there will be nothing left of any of us.

Ali

The evening after the women's protest, more reinforcements arrive in Timbuktu.

They have been arriving every night since the invasion, these truckloads of warriors from all over Muslim Africa. They come from Mauritania, from Guinea and Algeria, from Niger and Nigeria, from North Sudan and Chad. They park their vehicles outside the fort, armed to the teeth and zealous for the glory of God's name. Some of them are known to Redbeard from his years of Wahhabist wandering. Others are asked for proof of their jihadi credentials.

"Look around you!" Redbeard exclaims as he gets to his feet after night prayers. "What you see before you is the true United Nations. Not an amphitheater of gossips wearing curly microphones, but an army of saints wearing AK-47s, the finest city government on earth!"

I must be going. It's time for night patrol. I stand up painfully and head toward the gate.

As I walk past Redbeard, I can feel him looking at me. "Ali Konana!" he calls out. "Why so sad?"

Slowly I turn round to face him—not just him but the rows of kneeling fighters behind him.

"No reason," I say.

"Nonsense!" Redbeard jumps to his feet and strides toward me. "Tell me what's wrong."

The Ninjas, the foreigners, Muhammad Zaarib, all of them are looking at me now.

"It's that girl, master," I stutter. "She's only eleven."

Redbeard's forehead furrows. "I told you before, Ali. The whip will not kill her. It will teach her a lesson. A moment of discomfort for a lifetime of blessing."

"Right," I mutter.

"Right indeed." He strides toward me with open arms and gathers me into a tight embrace. "God disciplines us," he whispers in my ear, "like a father disciplines his sons. Never forget that, Ali."

Doesn't he realize everyone is watching us?

Doesn't he realize Fulani boys don't hug, not even their own fathers?

Doesn't he realize his rifle butt is sticking painfully into my side?

Despite all that, I don't want him to let go.

☾

Independence Square is dark and silent. I feel rags under my feet and the occasional clink of a spent shell. There is no insurgency afoot tonight, no overt rebellion against God's laws. The immediate crisis has passed, and the women of Timbuktu are learning to obey.

I draw my knife from its sheath on my belt and start to carve a spoon. Redbeard is right, of course. We need God's discipline.

Deep in my pocket my phone vibrates.

Climb the tree says the text.

I look up at the balustrade. She is standing there, veiled, phone in hand.

No.

I'll come down, then.

Don't.

It's too late. She swings her legs over the balustrade and reaches out to grab a sycamore branch.

"Stop it," I hiss. "You might fall."

Dark and formless in her veil, she propels herself along the branch and down into the heart of the tree. A parakeet bursts out of the foliage and flies away, squawking in irritation.

Kadi drops to the ground, lands awkwardly, and falls over backward.

I told her she would fall.

She gets up, smooths her crumpled veil, and crosses the street. I shine my flashlight at her as she walks toward me. The veil is dark and shapeless, as it should be, but on her feet are a pair of bright red shoes with pointy toes. Are shoes like that *haram*? If not, they should be.

"Hello, Abdullai," she says.

Abdullai. A wave of nausea hits me.

"Are you whittling a flute, Abdullai? I hear you make beautiful flutes. We could use a flute in our music group, you know."

I glance up the street toward the mosque. A group of boys come out of a side street and walk toward us with bundles of firewood on their heads. They must be on their way to a marabout's yard for a night of Qur'anic study. They have not seen us yet, but soon they will.

133

I slide my whittling knife into the sheath on my belt, grab Kadi's hand, and pull her behind the mechanic's shack. We listen as the boys pass by, and then the road is silent once again.

"How do you know those things?" I hiss. "Who have you been talking to?"

"I went to the Kabara Road Hospital to visit my friend Aisha. Do you remember her, Abdullai? Short hair, big eyes, incinerated kora? She got hurt in the stampede this afternoon, not that you would care. Anyway, on the mat next to Aisha there was this girl from Goundam. Very quiet, she was, what with her broken ribs, but her sisters talked a lot. I asked them if they know you, and they do."

"They don't," I say. "They know the boy I used to be. That's all."

"They say you're good at soccer, Abdullai. You play in goal for Goundam in the league."

"That was an age ago."

"Baba says goalkeepers are very brave," she whispers, stepping closer. "And a little bit crazy."

"Soccer is *haram*," I say.

"That's Ali speaking," she whispers, standing on tiptoes so that her warm breath tickles my ear. "It's Abdullai I want to talk to."

God knows I want to talk to her. I am entranced by her poisonous scent and her talk of flutes and goalkeeping. I am straining against my warrior name like a ram against a leash. My only desire, my only conscious thought, is to lift the Sufi's indigo veil and kiss her tattooed lips.

This nook behind the mechanic's shack is hidden from the street. One kiss, that's all, and nobody would know.

She leans toward me. Her fingers brush my belt and the sheath of my knife.

Be strong, I tell myself. *Whenever a boy is alone with a girl, the*

Devil makes a third. I step back hard against the wall of the shack, pressing myself against the corrugated tin so that my lash wounds scream in protest. I clench my jaw and press back harder still.

The pain is exquisite and divine. It racks my soul and brings me back to life.

"Abdullai is dead," I say, knocking her hand away. "My name is Ali."

"Ali! Ali! Why do you have to be Ali?" She bangs the corrugated tin. "So what if Redbeard gave you that name? Refuse it! Give it back to him!"

"It's more than just a name. It's who I am."

"Listen, Abdullai, the girls at the hospital also told me how much Redbeard is paying your family to have you fighting with them. For cattle herders it's an absolute fortune! You joined the Defenders because you love your parents. I understand that now."

"Nonsense!" I hiss. "Redbeard is more of a father to me than my own father ever was."

I stop, shocked at my own words. My father taught me almost nothing about God, but he did teach me about cows. Am I to despise him for that?

She backs away and slumps down on the ground. Her head is in her hands, her shoulders heave. I feel sorry for her.

"Feed the white horse," I tell her. "Don't feed the black horse, feed the white one."

"What?"

"We are all a blend of good and bad desires, Kadi, but our lives depend on which desires we feed. Feed the white horse, Kadi, and he will carry you to Paradise. And starve the black horse, lest he get strong and bear you off to—"

"Are you preaching to me?" says Kadi, springing to her feet. "How dare you preach to me, you of all people!"

"I'm trying to help you," I tell her. "From this night on, whenever you feed your father's horse, you will remember God, and the importance of—"

"Shut up!" she yells. "I don't need your stupid sermons. And for your information, I never feed my father's horse. I hate Marimba."

"Why? What has he ever done to you?"

"This," she says, and kicks me in the shins with her devilish red shoes.

I do not even flinch. Not because it doesn't hurt—it does—but because I don't want to give her the satisfaction.

Besides, something she just said jars my mind. It makes no sense.

"Are you sure?" I say slowly. "You never feed your father's horse?"

"Never, why?"

"Because the other morning, when I was in your yard, I saw your footprints in the horse's pen."

"You pig!" she cries. "I thought you came in to help me, not to spy on us."

"You went to the haystack and back," I say. "Is that where you keep the manuscripts? In the haystack?"

"What sort of imbecile keeps manuscripts in a haystack?" she cries. "Besides, who said anything about manuscripts? I told you, we've only got one manuscript."

"Your father seems to think you have more than one," I say.

"What?"

"'Kadija,'" I say, lowering my voice to imitate her father. "'How many times have I told you never to take manuscripts outside this house, yet you deliberately disobey me!'"

"He didn't say that!" She is desperate now. "He didn't!"

She turns and runs across the road and climbs the sycamore tree.

She's mad, that girl.

I sit down on my tire and rub my aching shins.

Manuscript 3,588: the tarikh of
Muhammad Fodiri Al-Wangari

Muhammad Fodiri Al-Wangari was traveling on foot from Timbuktu to Djenné, when he stopped for sunset prayer. He spread his cloak on the ground and stood on it to pray.

An infidel passed that way, saw Wangari's fine embroidered cloak, and decided to steal it. As the infidel reached out his hand, Fodiri Al-Wangari levitated three inches into the air so that the thief could snatch the cloak without disturbing his prayer.

The would-be thief converted there and then. He stood beside the airborne saint to weep, repent, and pray.

May the blessing of Muhammad Fodiri Al-Wangari be upon us.

Kadija

The day after the women's protest, Baba and Mama go to a naming ceremony near the old Sankore Mosque. Even in these desperate times, people still give babies names. They shave the baby's head and whisper in its ear the ninety-nine names of God.

Me, I'm home alone, preparing rice and mafé for the evening meal. Mafé is Baba's favorite sauce, but we hardly ever have it because it takes a whole afternoon to prepare.

POK-POK-POK, the spices smell divine. All fourteen famous spices of Timbuktu are congregated in this pounding pot: cinnamon sticks, bay leaves, cumin, aniseed, hibiscus, sumbala, onion flakes, black pepper, pitted dates, chili, sundried tomato, kabay lichen, wangaray seeds, and fine Taoudenni salt.

While I pound, I sing the first few verses of an old pounding ballad that Mama taught me—the ballad of Jali Madi. One day, or so the story goes, a young man called Jali Madi is running

139

after his fiancée when she disappears into a deep, dark cave. He follows her inside and finds to his horror that she has been captured by a djinni. "She must stay here forever with me," says the djinni, "but I'll give you something in return." And he gives Jali Madi an exquisite musical instrument with twenty-one strings, the world's first-ever kora.

I love sad songs these days. I feign a tremor in my voice and wield the pounding stick with wild grief. I wish the band were here to accompany me. We haven't played together since Tondi's wedding.

BING-BING, a text comes through. I reach for the phone. The song dies on my lips.

> Redbeard has an illuminated Al-Fatiha manuscript
> just like yours.

I lean on my pounding stick to steady myself, and the fourteen spices in my nostrils make me want to gag. Our Hausawi Al-Fatiha is utterly unique. Redbeard cannot have one the same. *Unless...*

I take down the jar of cinnamon sticks from the top shelf, unscrew the top, remove a key, and break into a run, spilling the precious spices with my trailing foot. Across the yard, over the fence, across the pen, I dash. Marimba startles and moves aside.

These are desperate times in Timbuktu. The rains are late, the banks are shuttered, and money's running short. Can it really be that Baba has sold a manuscript?

The key turns smoothly in the lock and I skedaddle down the earthen steps. I light the lamp, locate trunk twelve, and open up the lid. There it is, praise to the Lord of worlds, right where I left it. Whatever Redbeard has, it's not our Al-Fatiha.

"Peace be upon you," says a voice.

What have I done? Sweet saints of Timbuktu, what have I done?

Ali steps down onto the earthen floor of the vault and looks round him.

"Get out," I tell him. "My parents will be back soon."

"I think not." He is grinning like a pig in an open sewer. "No one leaves a naming ceremony early. They stay until the end, when the kola nuts are handed out."

"*Nyammu inna maa*," I mutter.

Fulani insults don't get much worse, but Ali feigns indifference. "Your veil was on your sleeping mat," he says, throwing it to me.

"You were on the roof?"

"Best spot for spying. Go on, put it on."

I throw the indigo fabric over my head. I am a rabbit in a burrow with a python. Powerless.

"Your message was stupid," I tell him. "Baba would never sell a manuscript. A collector in Bamako once offered thirty cows for the tarikh of Sidi Ahmed ben Amar. Thirty cows for one manuscript, and you know what Baba told him? It's not for sale!"

"And yet,"—Ali shrugs—"here you are."

Yes. Here I am. The witless daughter of a noble Guardian.

"I expected one trunk, maybe two," says Ali. "This is incredible."

"Turn around and leave," I say. "Forget what you have seen. I'm begging you, Abdullai."

"Don't call me that!" He strolls down the central aisle and marvels at the towering stacks of trunks. "Tell me, Kadija, how many manuscripts are in this chamber?"

"Twelve thousand. But only two thousand of those belong to us."

"Show me."

"Show you what?"

"I don't know. Your favorites."

141

My first instinct is to refuse. But then I remember Umar bin Said. I open the padlock of trunk sixteen and take out *The Mecca Letters*.

"Umar bin Said, ancient mystic." I lay the manuscript gently on the table and turn up the flame on the paraffin lamp. "He went on pilgrimage to Mecca and his journey took him through Bornu and Hausaland, two Muslim lands at war. It upset him so much to see Muslims fighting each other that he wrote this letter to both rulers."

Ali sighs and scans the page. "Think about your people . . . yakka-yakka . . . put aside your differences . . . yakka-yakka . . . Muslims should live together in peace . . . yakka-yakka . . . the end."

"You hardly looked at it," I say.

"I'm a fast reader," he says. "It's very nice."

"Very nice?" I stare at him. "Is that all you've got to say?"

"What else can I say? Peace between Muslims is good."

"Yet you attacked Timbuktu with guns and grenades?"

"It was full of idols."

"Killing is wrong, Ali."

"Did your father tell you that?"

"Yes."

Ali pushes back his chair. "Was that before or after he shot me in the back?"

I swallow drily.

"Kabyle muskets are very rare," drawls Ali. "You certainly never see them in Mali. Oh, wait, I'm wrong. There's one, on the wall."

"That's just a decoration," I say quickly.

He takes the musket down, opens the chamber, and sniffs. "Like I thought," he says. "Your father shot me."

"It wasn't Baba. It was me."

He holds me with a glittering eye. "Take off your veil, just for a moment."

142

"Why?"

"So I can see if you are lying."

"It would be improper," I tell him. "Anyway, if you were shot in the back, then how come you're not—"

"Dead?" Ali fishes in his pocket and pulls out the lemon-shaped ball I've seen him playing with at night.

It's not a ball. It's a grenade.

"My kit was in a leather bag on my back," he says. "Your musket ball went through the bag and into this." He rattles it and grins.

"If that's true, you're a very lucky boy."

"And you're a very brave girl." He replaces the musket on the wall. "Come on, let's see another manuscript."

I walk down the central aisle of the vault. The trunks tower above me to my left and right like walls of standing water. We do not have much time. Baba and Mama could come back any minute.

If Baba finds me in the vault with a Defender, my life is over. He will never let me take the Guardian's oath. Not ever.

At the end of the aisle are the writings of Ahmad Baba. Ahmad Baba taught for twenty years in Timbuktu, then fourteen years in Marrakesh as captive-guest of Sultan Al-Mansur. He returned to Mali, practiced law, and wrote a load of books. He was a humble man, Ahmad Baba, and the greatest scholar in the history of Timbuktu. If anyone can rescue Ali from the clutches of his henna-bearded Pharaoh, Ahmad Baba can.

"This one's good," I tell him, hurrying back to the table. "It's called *The Virtues of Scholarship*." I lay the manuscript before him and hover as he reads.

"Yakka-yakka," murmurs Ali. "The quest for knowledge is better than the waging of war . . . yakka-yakka . . . and on the Day of—"

There is a sudden catch in his voice. He stops abruptly.

"What is it?" I ask. "What's wrong?"

Ali takes a deep breath. "He says that on the Day of Judgment the in—"

He halts again, and a tear rolls down his cheek.

Fulani boys don't cry.

"Don't worry, Ali." I lay a hand on his shoulder. "Tears are a gift from God. Let them come."

He takes a shallow breath and reads aloud. "*On the Day of Judgment the ink of the scholars will be measured against the blood of the martyrs, and found to be weightier.*"

He is desperate not to cry but the tears insist.

"Let them come," I repeat. "Repentance is a holy thing, Ali."

He tries to speak, but his torso is racked by a sudden violent sob. I hug him from behind and he surrenders to his anguish. His face is buried in his arms, my arms are round his neck, and intertwined we ride the pain of his despair.

"*If anyone repents after his wrongdoing and puts things right,*" I quote, "*then God will turn toward him, for God is Ever-Forgiving, Most Merciful.*"

"Shut up," snarls Ali.

"What?"

"This is not repentance. It's anger." He thumps *The Virtues of Scholarship*, billowing dust. "What does this scribbling whitebeard know about the blood of martyrs? How dare he compare himself to them? What does he know about passion or sacrifice? Nothing at all! One drop of Hilal's or Omar's blood weighs more than all the manuscripts in Timbuktu."

Ali yanks the metal lever on the lamp to raise the clear glass chimney and expose the orange flame.

"What are you doing?" I gasp. "Ali, no!"

144

He picks up the manuscript and shoves one corner into the flame. It curls and blackens.

I seize his wrists and pull with all my strength, inching the precious paper away from the fire. Ali stands up, knocking over the chair, and lunges forward again, determined to burn the manuscript. The next thing I know, I'm on his back with my legs round his waist, one hand over his eyes and the other reaching for the manuscript. He staggers away from the lamp, leans slightly to one side, swings a leg, and lets the priceless sheaf fall onto the arch of his foot as if he's punting a ball. *The Virtues of Scholarship* connects with the ex-goalkeeper's foot and explodes in a shower of paper fragments, dust, and termites.

"*A hanyan!*" I scream.

I kick his supporting leg just behind the knee, and he crumples facedown to the floor. My legs straddle his waist and my forearm is across the back of his neck, pinning him to the ground. I cannot call for help because my phone is on the table. With my free hand I reach for the chair to hit him with. My animal sobs echo off the trunks and earthen walls.

The chair is beyond my reach, and now I am off balance. Ali bucks his hips, then twists, and rolls me over so I'm lying on the ground and he is on top of me.

My hands are on his back, raking his lash wounds with my nails. He gasps in pain, slumps forward, and bites me on the neck to make me stop.

I do stop. So does he. His body stiffens. The taste of my blood has shocked him. We lie interlocked on the earth floor, and the only sound in the vault is our breathing, and the only thing between us is my veil.

I look up at him. The cuts on his face and chin from Tondi's wedding night are healing well, and the hardness in his gaze is gone. My abdomen is full of tuning rings that tighten more and more the longer we lie like this.

"Kadi," he whispers.

"Abdullai." I lift my head and kiss him through my cotton veil.

I can feel his cantering heartbeat through my dress. His lips respond to mine, uncertainly at first and then with confidence. Fragments of Ahmad Baba rustle and crunch beneath us.

One of his hands is under my head and the other moves down to unclasp my hijab pin but even when the veil is cast aside my face still burns for he is kissing my lips and my cheeks and the curls on my temples and the bite marks on my neck. We are no longer Jihadist or Sufi or invader or invaded, for those barriers have gone. He is Abdullai the herder boy and I am Kadija the almost beautiful and Timbuktu is any far-off place, and by the time we hear my cousin's footsteps we are inextricable.

A quavery voice from the steps: "Kadi, are you all right?"

I know how it must look, this awful scene—the chair knocked over, the manuscript scattered to the four corners of the vault, the terrified librarian flailing underneath the warrior.

"Yusuf! Help me! Get him off me!"

Abdullai stares at me. The confusion in his eyes gives way to hurt, the agony of betrayal. *Kadi, what did you just say? What have you done to me?* And then his features harden, and Abdullai is gone, perhaps forever.

Cousin Yusuf strides across the vault, grabs the fallen chair, and smashes it on Ali's back. The warrior grunts in pain and rolls off onto the floor. Yusuf reaches down and pulls the knife from Ali's belt, a slender blade glinting orange in the lamp-light.

The Defender stumbles to his feet, wild-eyed, unarmed. He staggers to the end of the aisle, where deep blue trunks loom

146

sternly on both sides to hem him in. Like Pharaoh's soldiers in the Sea of Reeds, Ali is trapped.

Yusuf advances on him slowly with the knife.

"Yusuf, don't," I say. "If you hurt him, Redbeard and the others will kill you."

"I'll take that chance," Yusuf snarls.

Casting around for a weapon, Ali spots the iron padlock on the top of trunk sixteen. He lifts it, feels its weight, and flings it hard. By a single span it misses Yusuf's head.

Yusuf grins. "Ninja, you're losing your touch."

But Yusuf was not the Ninja's target. There comes a clang of metal and a splintering of glass, and all goes dark.

I can hear Yusuf's footsteps running up the aisle and the clang of his fists against the metal trunks. "Come here, coward!" he shouts, but his own voice too is tight with fear. "Where are you? Where've you gone?"

"Yusuf, your phone!" I shout, whilst feeling on the table for my own.

"Got it," he says, and his backlight comes on.

The aisle is empty, and so is the rest of the vault. I hear the creak of the ancient door above, and the quiet clunk of the key in the lock.

Yusuf charges up the steps.

"He's locked us in!" he cries.

And that is that.

The Virtues of Scholarship is broken beyond repair, and so is Baba's office chair, and so am I.

Ali

I pocket the key to the secret door and storm into the street, wiping my sleeve across my stupid lips, while Redbeard's warnings echo in my head. *Put a man in the desert with only his Book and his gun, and he will easily master himself. But make that man a ruler of one of the greatest cities on earth and his worldly self will rise again. In the coming days and weeks, you will be tempted in every way, but you must not give in.*

He warned us to be careful, yet still I fell for her. I fell for the radiance of her Al-Fatiha, her come-hither texts, and her *haram* perfume. I fell for her impudence, her lazy eyelids, and her part-time veil.

I fell in flame like Lucifer from heaven.

I stride along Askia Street. The midday glare assaults my eyes. No shadows at this time of day, not even from the lofty turrets of the Djinguereber Mosque. No relief.

I'm furious at the Sufi for seducing and betraying me. Furious at myself for letting it happen. Furious at the so-called saints of Timbuktu, the shrines, the manuscripts, the superstitions, and every other nonsense that distracts a city from its God.

A Somali mujahid with a scar along one cheek is guarding the gate of the camp today. "What's wrong?" he asks as I approach. "You look like a rhino on *bleu-bleu* tablets."

I ignore him and storm into the camp. Off-duty fighters lounge and loll, clipping their nails, sleeping, brewing ginger tea.

Jabir is stripping his rifle. As soon as he sees my face, his eyes widen in surprise and sympathy. "What happened?" he asks.

"Nothing," I snap. "Where are the pickaxes?"

He points with his chin.

I grab a pickaxe and cross the compound to the tomb of Tamba-Tamba. We should have done this long ago.

"God is great!" I cry, and swing the axe.

The head of the pickaxe buries itself in the wall right up to the handle.

That's for you, Kadija.

I lock my elbows and pull the axe toward me. The tomb wall bulges and cracks. A slab of earth falls at my feet.

That's for you, old women. Now where will you go to chant your detestable chants?

I swing the pickaxe again, a few meters to the left of my first hole. The axe lodges in the bricks and emerges with a dry crunch, bringing with it another large section of the wall.

That's for flabby-minded Sufis everywhere.

The two holes in the wall of the tomb gape at me like the eye sockets of a skull. A phrase from my childhood comes into my mind: *Do not disturb the spirits in their eternal rest, for the spirits never forgive.*

I shoo the thought away. This is Tamba-Tamba, after all, the man of righteous anger, who in his fury stamped a foot-shaped hole one furlong deep. Imagine his wrath at six centuries of idolatry committed in his name. Unless I desecrate his resting place, he'll get no rest at all.

I drop the pickaxe and launch a flying kick at the wall between the two holes. It crumbles, and the section above it drops as well.

I spring back from the tumbling masonry.

"*Alhamdulillah!*" The voice behind me is Redbeard's. "That's right, brave Ali, rage against the idols!"

Again I lift the axe and drive its unforgiving nose into the brickwork of the tomb. My fury gives me supernatural strength. I could demolish this abominable tomb with my bare hands if I needed to.

Redbeard is beside me now, to aid the demolition. He swings his axe with savage elation, working his way round the shrine, slicing it open like a tin of fish.

Warriors from all over the world converge upon the tomb with axes, shovels, rifle butts, hoes, and hands and feet.

Tamba-Tamba is his name, and that is how we smash his tomb. Fast-fast.

☽

I have started something extraordinary, something holy and frightening, something that I could not stop even if I wanted to.

Out of the gates of the camp we burst into Independence Square. Al Farouk, the city's failed protector, regards us from his saddle with a gimlet eye. We stream toward him, furious.

For today is Judgment Day in Timbuktu.

For there is no god but God.

For Al Farouk must die.

Muhammad Zaarib wins the race and mounts the pedestal,

swings high his bifurcated sword, and smites the djinni's throat. Our ferocious cheer echoes off the prim facades of the town hall, the police station, and the Sidi Yahya Mosque.

Zaarib picks up the head and raises it aloft. "God is great!" he cries.

We leave the headless horseman in the square and swarm up Askia Street, drunk with holy passion, through the nomad camp and toward the Cemetery of the Three, where stand the famous tombs of Muhammad Mahmoud, Sidi Mohamed al Miky, and Sidi Ahmed ben Amar.

Before the tomb of ben Amar, a group of pilgrims whirl.

> *"We entreat your blessing, Sidi Ahmed ben Amar,*
> *Son of Sidi el Wafi, son of Sidi el Moctar,*
> *For daily salt we beg thee, Sidi Ahmed ben Amar,*
> *Let the heavens rain down on us."*

The stupid Sufis open their eyes and find themselves surrounded. The whirling and the singing stop.

"Leave," I tell them.

The tomb of Sidi Ahmed ben Amar is covered with pieces of white cloth to represent the slabs of heavenly salt. Aghast, the pilgrims watch us as we tear the cloths to shreds and attack the shrine with hoes and axes.

Jabir climbs onto my shoulders and onto the roof of the tomb. I throw him a pickaxe and he smashes a hole in the roof, starting in the middle and working outward. For the first time in six hundred years, a ray of sunlight shines into the tomb of Sidi Ahmed ben Amar.

A crowd is gathering. All of Timbuktu, it seems, is arriving at the Cemetery of the Three. Young men pour through the gates with soccer shirts and fists clenched tight. Clouds of veiled women billow in behind them. Even the whitebeards are gathering up their robes and running.

The mayor is also on the scene, as fat and impotent as ever. Jowls wobbling, prayer beads clicking, he picks his way through the rubble to where Redbeard stands.

"This is a crime!" yells the mayor. "It is a crime against the city, a crime against culture, a crime against humanity!"

"But not against God," replies Redbeard. "Stand back, *Monsieur le Maire*, or you are going to get hurt."

The mayor does not budge. He is livid, and so are the people in the crowd. I do not expect them to understand. We are loosing their chains and setting free their souls, but they cannot see it. Their eyes are blinded by the Evil One.

A young man in a Rasta hat bends down, picks up a stone, and flings it hard at Jabir on the roof. Redbeard tuts, and shrugs his AK-47 off his shoulder. He fires into the air on full auto and watches the petrified crowd shrink back. He discards the old magazine, inserts a fresh one, and yanks the bolt handle to the rear in readiness. There he stands, Akka the Great of Mauritania, so skillful with an AK that they named him after it. Nobody in Timbuktu is going to save this tomb.

At last, the fatal blow is struck. The east wall of the tomb collapses outwards and the roof caves in.

"Jabir!" I cry. "Are you OK?"

He rises dusty faced from the rubble and gives me two thumbs-up.

We surge into the tomb, clear the fallen earth off Sidi Ahmed's grave, and start to dig.

The mayor emits a leonine roar. "Not the body!" he yells. "Don't you *dare* bring up the body!"

We bring the body up into the light, first a dirty rib cage dangling from a shovel and then the real prize, the grinning skull, which Zaarib holds up high for all to see.

"Behold your saint!" he shouts.

The men of Timbuktu surge forward to avenge the desecration, but Redbeard lifts his AK-47 again and fires over their heads—another hail of bullets and another quick reload.

"Can a carcass answer prayer?" cries Redbeard. "Can a skull give salt? Oh, look, here comes a pelvis on a spade, a sorry sight indeed. I half expected it to glow with the *noor* of God himself, but look how dark it is, and rotten. Even the wildest dog in Timbuktu would wrinkle up its nose at such a bone!"

The veiled women caterwaul and weep, a wretched backing track to Redbeard's rant. And all the while, shoulder to shoulder with my brothers, giddy with iconoclastic joy, I swing my axe. When we are done here, we will destroy the tomb of Alpha Moya, protector of the east, then Sidi el Moctar, protector of the north, then all the other saints of Timbuktu. And finally, with the eyes of the whole world upon us, we will visit the tomb of that inking, blinking, weak-chinned scribbler, Ahmad Baba himself. On behalf of Hilal and Omar, I will grind his tomb to dust, and prove that passion, sweat, and blood can accomplish what the watery ink of scholars never could: the worship of the one true God in Timbuktu.

The sun's bright rays slant low into the tomb, and still our axes plow the salt saint's grave. We shatter femurs, shoulder blades, and ribs, and then—at last, a real horror—my pickaxe meets a bone less brittle than the rest.

I hear a nauseating crack and a wheeze of pain, and shielding my eyes from the setting sun, I see a turbaned man writhing on the ground, clutching his leg.

I swear, I didn't see him. I didn't mean to hit him. Where in God's name did he come from, this loon in starched, white robes?

Redbeard comes over and loosens the man's turban to help him breathe.

"*Astaghfirullah,*" I gasp.

It's Kadija's father.

Kadija

Yusuf has no credit on his phone, and I have enough for just one text.

Come to the vault, Mama. We're locked in.

I wait in the darkness beside the door. My cousin stays down in the vault. "It would be improper," he says, "for us to be together in the dark."

I can guess the real reason, though. He's in shock and wants to cry.

Mama arrives at last and we shout at each other through the heavy door. She asks questions and I tell half-truths. "I went to the vault to look for that ancient Mafé recipe of yours, Mama. A Defender was spying on me from the roof. He followed me, Mama."

"Purity of God!" cries Mama. "Did he hurt you?"

"No, Mama. Yusuf turned up just in time."

I don't tell her about the kiss. She wouldn't understand.

How could she? Even I don't understand.

"I'll get your father and Uncle Abdel," says Mama. "There was some commotion at the Cemetery of the Three, and they went to take a look."

She hurries off, leaving me in the narrow hallway at the top of the steps. A single beam of light shines through the keyhole, alive with specks of dancing dust.

"Yusuf!" I shout. "Come here."

He hurries up the steps.

"Why did you come here, Yusuf?"

"You just told me to."

"No, earlier I mean, when you found us in the vault together."

"I heard you scream," he says uncertainly.

"I see."

"Did he—" Yusuf hesitates. "Did he hurt you?"

"No, thanks to you. But he certainly hurt *The Virtues of Scholarship*."

"It's terrible," says Yusuf. "For someone who preaches that soccer is forbidden, he has an excellent half volley."

"Yes."

I reach for his hand. Our fingers intertwine.

"I should go back down to the vault," says Yusuf thickly.

"Wait."

Still holding his hand, I step toward him and twist his arm up behind his back.

"Ouch!" he cries. "What are you doing?"

"How do you know he kicked it, Yusuf?"

"What do you mean?" He gives a short, light laugh. Too short, and much too light.

"How do you know that he kicked the manuscript?" I am speaking slowly, as if to an imbecile. "I never told you he kicked it."

"I saw him. Hey! I saw him!"

I push his hand farther up his back until I feel the strain on all three of the joints in his arm. "You said you came because you heard me scream, Yusuf. But I only screamed because he kicked the manuscript. *You can't have seen him kick the manuscript, Yusuf. It's impossible.*"

"I remember," he gasps. "I saw part of a footprint on one of the manuscript fragments."

"You must think I'm an idiot," I snarl, and yank his hand right up between his shoulder blades.

"Please, Kadi! That really hurts!" He is standing on tiptoes, trying to ease the pain.

"There are a lot of broken bones in the Kabara Road Hospital at the moment," I say. "I hear they are running out of supplies to treat them all."

"I'll tell you, I'll tell you," Yusuf whimpers. "I'll tell you everything." I ease the pressure on his arm, and my cousin sighs like a deflating tire. "I like you, Kadi, though only God knows why. And I've been—" he hesitates. "I've been watching you. There is something you don't know about this vault. Something no one knows but me."

Ali

Twelve tombs in ten hours. Our bodies are tired, but our spirits are still eager to do the will of God. Is there a cemetery we have not yet visited, a saint whose bones lie undisturbed?

There are no more shrines to smash, but there is, of course, one idol left.

"Come, Ali Konana, let's finish this thing," says Redbeard, throwing me an AK-47 magazine belt. "We'll go to the Sidi Yahya Mosque, just you and me. We have an ancient mystery to solve."

Just you and me. What an honor. I feel like the Ali of old, protecting his lord at the Battle of Uhud. I strap the belt round my waist and fit a magazine in every pouch. There's anger in Timbuktu tonight; we need to go prepared.

On the way to the mosque, I keep thinking about Kadija's father. They loaded him onto the back of a donkey cart like an injured cow, and off he went to the Kabara Road Hospital, and he was looking at me as he went. Not saying anything, just looking.

What kind of demons possess a man to jump in front of a swinging axe? It's not normal. He has only his demons to blame.

By the time we arrive at the mosque, it is past ten o'clock and the night prayer crowd has already dispersed. In the inner courtyard, six Qur'anic students are writing and reciting by a fire. Imam Cissé sits on a mat nearby, shrouded in a thick blanket. He looks up when we arrive and points a spindly finger at Redbeard.

"The crimes you have committed today," croaks the imam, "will be visited on you a thousandfold in the hereafter."

Redbeard ignores the threat and wanders to the ancient wooden door on the east side of the compound. Its silver suns, moons, and stars sparkle in the light of the fire.

"Tell me about this door," he says.

Imam Cissé shrugs off his blanket and leans on his walking stick to help him stand. "Stay away from that door. Do you hear me, Ould Hamaha? If you so much as touch that door, I will kill you myself."

"You, boy." Redbeard points at one of the imam's students. "Tell me about the door."

The teenager hesitates, then gabbles his answer all in one breath. "It's a very special door," he says. "It will not open until the end of the world when the Prophet Musa calls the Prophet Isa to come and judge the world, and those whose works were pleasing to God will go through that door and enter into their rest because it is the Door of Heaven."

Redbeard spits in the sand. "Are you telling me," he says, "that heaven is on the other side of this door?"

"Yes," squeaks the student.

"I can't wait to see it," says Redbeard. "After you, Ali."

"No!" cries Imam Cissé.

I raise my pickaxe above my head and bring it down hard on the Door. The axe head glances off an ornate silver sun. I swing again. This time it hits a moon, rebounds, and strikes me on the shoulder.

"*Alhamdulillah!*" cries Imam Cissé. "You see, it can't be done!"

He's wrong. It can be done. The rivets of these ancient doors were designed to resist attack, but everything has a weakness.

For my third strike I pick my spot more carefully, aiming at the seam between two central panels. The pickaxe lands, the wood splits open, and the head of my axe lodges so deeply in the door that I cannot pull it out. Redbeard throws me his axe, and I land another blow, and then another. The panels start to fall apart and shed their silver rivets.

It is the beginning of the End. Moons and stars tumble through space and drop like silver petals on the sand.

"Purity of God!" cries Imam Cissé. "Stop, I beg you!"

I carry on till all eleven panels of the so-called Door of Heaven lie smashed and splintered on the ground.

Redbeard shines his flashlight into the darkness beyond. Heaven is a windowless mud-brick room, completely empty but for dust, cobwebs, and a small black scorpion.

The scorpion scuttles out, its tail arched, and heads heroically for Redbeard's foot.

Redbeard bends, grasps the scorpion by its sting, and scowls at it. "I was expecting the Prophet Isa, not you," he whispers to the flailing arachnid. "I must say, I am disappointed."

He snaps off the sting, drops the scorpion on the ground, lets it skitter a little way, then stamps on it.

Imam Cissé is staring at the broken door. He clasps the head of his walking stick so tight his knuckles whiten. "Curse you, curse you both," he says, in a peculiar, reedy voice. "May God command the desert djinn to smite you from the earth and wing you to the place where you belong."

On a nail next to the Door of Heaven hangs a goatskin water pouch. Redbeard unhooks the pouch and offers it to the old man.

"Come, father, you should follow the example of Imam Karim. Seek refuge from your anger. Lie down, make yourself comfortable on the sand, and allow me to pour some water over you."

The imam does not lie down. He strides toward Redbeard holding his walking stick in both hands, and then, with a sudden twist of the wrists, the walking stick comes apart.

I gasp out loud. The shaft of the imam's stick is a hollow wooden sheath, and its sculpted handle the hilt of a sword—a sword which even now is swinging through the air toward the mujahid.

Redbeard lifts the goatskin pouch to defend himself. Scant defense. The imam's sword slices cleanly through the leather, and the water bursts out, drenching my master's hair and henna beard.

Cissé plants his feet and lifts the silver sword again. This is no time to stand and stare. I have to act. Like Ali of old, I must protect my lord.

I drop to one knee, grab a handful of sand, and fling it in the imam's angry eyes.

The old man blinks and staggers, and my master takes his chance to move in for the kill.

No, not for the kill. He has more class than that. As Imam Cissé blindly swings his sword, the mujahid leaps to one side and delivers a lightning knuckle punch to the outside of the imam's sword arm, just below his elbow.

161

The sword falls to the ground, the imam to his knees.

The Qur'anic students are on their feet. They're picking up firebrands and bits of broken door, but by the time they get within five meters of us, our guns are leveled at their chests.

"Come on, boys!" bawls Redbeard. "Which one of you is first?"

None of them, it seems. They drop their weapons and back away, their hands above their heads.

"I can't move my fingers," Imam Cissé whines. "What have you done to me, Ould Hamaha?"

"I struck your radial nerve. Don't worry, old man, the paralysis is only temporary."

"You there!" I point to one of the Qur'anic students. "Go and find some water to wash the sand out of your teacher's eyes."

Redbeard sheathes the imam's silver sword and holds it up to look at it. "Exquisite," he says, shaking his head. "The seam is completely invisible. I'll buy it."

"It's not for sale," the imam snaps.

Redbeard counts out a wad of purple notes. "Here's fifty thousand to repair your door, and thirty thousand for your walking stick."

"Keep your cursed money."

My master slides the rolled-up notes into the imam's hand, then turns and walks away. "Too bad," he calls back. "A man who cannot move his fingers must accept what he is given!"

My master and I swagger side by side through Independence Square, taking turns with the imam's silver sword. We're drunk with holy victory and desperate for more.

The shrines are smashed. The Door is down. I imagined that would be enough.

It's not, of course.

How could it be enough, when those repulsive manuscripts remain? They are lying there right now, intact and gloating in their vault with Kadi and her stupid cousin. The manuscripts are the curse of Timbuktu, an insult to the memory of the martyrs. Soft books, every one of them, infecting Sufi heads with fairy tales and stirring sick hearts with desire.

I managed to destroy one manuscript this afternoon. Twelve thousand more remain.

"Ali Konana, you did well back there," says Redbeard. "The way you improvised and threw that sand. It was masterly."

"It was nothing," I mumble.

"Nonsense!" he cries, lunging at thin air with the imam's sword. "Your quick thinking saved my life! As of this moment, you're my favorite son."

"Thank you," I mumble.

"God gave us victory today," Redbeard declares, "and tonight the city of Timbuktu is free of superstition."

"No, master, it's not," I hear myself say.

It is the first time ever that I have contradicted Redbeard. A soldier never contradicts, but a favorite son is different.

"Go on," he says. "I'm listening."

◟

By the time we reach Askia Street, I am already wishing I had not told Redbeard about Kadi's manuscripts. My head tells me it's right to destroy them, but my heart is not so sure.

The front door to Kadi's compound is bolted from the inside.

"There's no way in," I say.

Redbeard just laughs and points at the sycamore tree. We climb the tree and hop onto the roof.

The roof and the compound below are dark and silent.

We drop down into the courtyard and hop over the fence into

the horse's pen. The father's stallion is standing by the wall. It gazes as we pass.

There behind the hay bales is the door. I had expected the lock to be smashed, but there is no sign of damage. None at all.

I borrow Redbeard's flashlight and shine it on the sand. Going to and from the door are Mama Diallo's sharp-toed footprints. And here are the tracks of Kadi and her cousin, leading *to* the door, *but not away.*

Strange. I breathe. *They're still inside.*

I take the key from my pocket and turn it in the lock.

As soon as I open the door, I smell smoke.

"*Salaam alaikum,*" I call.

No answer.

Pulse pounding in my ears, I step across the threshold and shine the flashlight down the steps. I cannot see the whole vault, only the narrow section at the foot of the steps. But what I see there makes my stomach churn.

A pile of ash lies by the wall, gray ash and blackened stumps. Toward the outer edge of the ash lie the charred remains of two red shoes and an indigo veil.

"Purity of God!" I cry, running down the steps toward the bodies.

Too late I notice a pair of silver rivets pressed into the wall on either side of the staircase. Too late I notice a kora string stretched low between them. My leading foot snags on the trip wire and I tumble down the steps, cracking my head on the floor of the vault.

In a burst of color on my eyelids I see the ruins of La Détente, the dancing flames, and broken instruments. I see black-lipped, furious faces. And lying on the sand, a kora string and two stray rivets. *Keep these as a souvenir*, I mouth. *God does not want your music. He wants your heart.*

"Are you all right?" shouts Redbeard.

"I don't know."

I lift myself up on one elbow and wince in pain. *Damn you, Kadi.*

Redbeard picks up his flashlight and shines it on the ash. "Those aren't bones," he says. "They're table legs. Why have they burned the furniture?"

"I don't know, master."

He shines his flashlight across the walls and ceiling. I don't believe it. The vault is void. Even the bookcase stands empty.

"Where are the trunks, Ali?"

I slump back to the floor. "I'm sorry, master. I don't know."

Kadija

The Kabara Road Hospital is still full of women. Even the men's wards are full of women. They have put Baba on a mat on the floor of a cleaning cupboard, surrounded by brooms and packets of Omo cleaning powder.

Baba and Mama are reciting *dhikr*, but they stop when they hear me come in.

"*Foofo*, Kadija," says Baba weakly.

The cleaning cupboard is surprisingly dirty. There are cobwebs on the ceiling, patches of bare plaster on the walls, and disgusting stains on the floor. It smells of bleach and decay.

"How is the patient?" I say, squatting down in a thicket of brooms and shining a flashlight at the broken leg. The bones have been realigned, dressed in a yellowing bandage, and strapped to a crude splint.

"The hospital has run out of plaster," says Mama, lighting a paraffin lamp. "And painkillers."

"*Dhikr* is my painkillers," says Baba with a tight smile. "But the healing will take time, they say. I could be here for weeks."

I exchange a look with Mama.

"Have you told him yet?" I whisper.

She shakes her head.

"Told me what?" my father says.

"We've got a problem," I say. "There was a Defender in the vault this afternoon."

"No!" My father tries to sit up, then slumps back down in pain. "How? What happened?"

I repeat the same story I told Mama. The ancient Mafé recipe. The Defender on the roof. The confrontation.

"Did he hurt you?" asks Baba.

"No."

"Does he know what's in the trunks?"

"Yes."

"Then the manuscripts are in danger!" Baba cranes his neck toward me, his eyes straining out of his head. "We must contact Abdel. We must call the horsemen of the sun. We must move the trunks again!"

"I've done it, Baba. They are out of the vault, but it's not enough. We need to get them out of Timbuktu."

"That decision is not yours to make!" snaps Baba. The pain and stress are getting to him. "It's mine!"

I look at Mama, and she gives another tiny nod. *It's time.*

"Baba," I say. "I want to take the oath."

"No," he says. "Absolutely not."

"Come on, Baba, we have no choice."

"She's right," says Mama. "There is nothing you and I can do, stuck in this cursed cupboard. Kadija loves those manuscripts, and she is clever too. She will make an excellent Guardian."

167

"In the name of God, the Compassionate and Merciful," I begin.

"Kadi, no."

"I solemnly swear to guard the manuscripts of Timbuktu entrusted to my family by the saints of old."

"Kadi, you are only fifteen. It's far too young."

"I will protect them in times of peace and in times of war, in times of planting and in times of harvesting, in times of joy and in times of sorrow. I will protect them from fire and from flood, from wizards and from thieves, from giants and from djinn."

The words pour from me like water from Sababou. I am a thing possessed. If the ceiling of the cleaning cupboard were to fall on me this second, every drop of my blood would be inscribed with the words of the oath.

"God grant me the wisdom of the horse, the stubbornness of the ox, and the cunning of the rabbit. God hide the manuscripts from every evil eye, and reveal them to every seeker of truth. From this moment, let wisdom be my only treasure and the legacy of the saints my only true delight. And this covenant now made on earth, may it be ratified in heaven."

Never in my life have I seen Baba cry, but his tears are flowing now, streaming over his craggy face and salt-and-pepper beard, and dripping on the mat.

Mama strokes his hair. "Peace, peace," she says, as if comforting a small child. "The manuscripts are safe with Kadi."

"Good night," I say. "I will come again tomorrow, *inshallah*."

I go out into the dark corridor, and then poke my head back in.

"Baba," I say. "Do you have a telephone number for Tijani Traoré, the ferryman?"

"Yes," says Baba. "Why?"

"I'm going to need a boat with a cargo deck big enough for all five hundred trunks."

Manuscript 8,736: the tarikh of Abu Alkassim Attouatti

Abu Alkassim Attouatti was an imam of the Djinguereber Mosque. He lived right next to the mosque and devoted his life to God and to scholarship. Imam Abu's pockets were the deepest in Timbuktu. He had many Qur'anic students and he lavished dates and bread on them. No matter how much he gave to one student, he always had enough for the next. And no matter what time of day it happened to be, the bread he gave them was always hot and fresh. No one ever found out how the freshly baked bread got into the imam's pockets.

One day, Imam Abu and his students went to the mosque to pray. When they straightened up after Tashahhud, one of his students noticed that the saint's robe was dripping with water.

"Imam Abu," cried the student. "When we began to pray, your robe was dry, and now it is wet through! What happened?"

"I have been on a journey," said Imam Abu. "A boatful of fishermen capsized in Lake Débo just now, and the fishermen began to drown. One of them called out in the name of God and his saints, so God sent me to save them. Don't look so scared, my friends. The fishermen are fine. They are home and fed and sitting by the fire to dry out."

"But Lake Débo is more than three days' travel from here!" protested the student. "How were you able to travel so far, so fast?"

Imam Abu smiled a peculiar smile. "In God's world," he whispered, "there are many mysterious things."

Ali

"There must be a spare key for that door up there," says Red-beard. "They let themselves out and they took the manuscripts with them."

"Impossible," I say. "We would have seen their tracks."

"Perhaps they covered their tracks."

I can't help smiling at that. If my master were Fulani, he would know how hard it is to cover tracks.

Redbeard clenches his fists. "Are you laughing at me, boy?"

"No, master."

We walk around the vault for a fourth time, shining the flashlight on every inch of earth. We run our hands over the walls, feeling for a crack, a lever, anything.

Nothing.

We drag the bookcase away from the north wall, and shine the flashlight into the gap. One loose manuscript folio has fallen down behind the bookcase—mislaid months ago, judging by the thick dust on it—but there is no trapdoor or tunnel, nothing to shed light on the mystery at hand.

"It's the fire that bothers me," says Redbeard, poking the ashes with his foot. "Why did they lay a fire?"

"I don't know, master."

"Come on!" he cries. "Why do people build fires?"

"To destroy things," I say. "Or to cook on."

"Yes, what else?"

"To keep warm on cold nights. To make charcoal. Or to dry out after getting wet."

To dry out after getting wet. I stare at the soot-blackened wall above the fire and think of all those nights I spent on patrol. All those hours sitting on my tire, gazing at two whitewashed villas with identical arched entrances and identical balustrades. Two brothers in two houses, each built to the same design . . .

"I know why they made the fire," I say at last. "They made it to dry the wall."

Redbeard looks at the wall and then at me. A slow grin lights his grizzled face.

We hurry to the bookcase and lean it slowly back until we are carrying it doors up. On the count of three we accelerate across the floor of the vault and ram it hard into the soot-blackened wall.

A section of the wall collapses with a loud crunch, and a shower of rubble patters down into the space beyond.

"*Allahu Akbar,*" Redbeard breathes.

I was right. The two villas were built to the same design, not just above ground but below as well. Two villas and two vaults, separated by a mud-brick wall. A wall plastered with mud to resemble solid earth.

We grab our guns and clamber through the hole.

The second vault is an exact reflection of Kadija's, and it is empty, except for a muddy hoe on the ground.

"Look," says Redbeard. "That's where they mixed the mortar to repair the hole."

I run up the earthen steps, but there is no door at the top, just a forest of cobwebs and a solid mud-brick wall. This vault has been blocked off for a long, long time. *So how did they get out of here?*

Confused, I head back down the steps.

Redbeard is standing in the middle of the vault, his flashlight pointing up at the ceiling.

"Look," he says. "Look there."

Directly above my master's head I see a square trapdoor. *Alhamdulillah!*

The trapdoor is the final piece of the puzzle, and in an instant I see how the trick was done.

I see them using table legs to smash their way into the vault where now I stand. I see Kadija shinnying up a rope through that trapdoor to summon her outlaw friends. I see a small army of workers coming down to help them, passing manuscript trunks through the hole in the wall and hauling them up through the trapdoor on some sort of stretcher. I see them gathering up the rubble, mixing a wet mud mortar, and blocking up the hole in the dividing wall. I see Kadija taking off her kora string necklace and setting a trip wire on the steps to punish the first intruder.

And then what? When you build a mud-brick wall in the open air, the hot sun dries the mortar in minutes. Underground, however, mud stays wet for ages. The repaired area would be darker than the rest of the wall and I would have spotted it straightaway. So they set a fire against the wall, using the table and chair legs and a liter or two of gasoline. Adding the shoes and veil would have been Kadija's idea—a shocking addition to the scene.

The finishing touches must have been tricky, of course, and delicately done. I see Kadija slipping her slim arm through the one remaining slot, and using wet fingers to smooth the plaster on the other side. I see her drawing back her hand for as long as it takes to light a match, then reaching through again to drop the flame onto the fuel-soaked wood.

I see Yusuf slapping mortar and plaster onto one final brick and thrusting it into the waiting slot. I imagine him turning to Kadija in the darkness and looping his arms around her waist.

We Fulani always end up marrying our cousins. It's what Fulani do.

Kadija

The night is dark. I perch with Cousin Yusuf on the roof of Al Haji's cattle truck. The driver has picked a winding off-road route behind the Cemetery of the Three and far out west beyond the nomad camps. Out here in the bush, there won't be any checkpoints, *inshallah*.

"I still don't get it," I tell my cousin. "Don't your parents know there's a vault beneath your house?"

"Of course they do," says Yusuf. "I remember my father telling me once, when I was very small. But the doorway to the vault was blocked up many generations ago and he never bothered to unblock it. He never needed to."

We turn and judder south across a rocky plateau, the truck's suspension creaking and clanking under the weight of five hundred metal trunks. I can't wait to reach the Kabara port, to get these manuscripts on the river and away from here.

"What about the trapdoor in your room?" I say. "Do your parents know about that?"

"No."

"Why did you dig it?"

"Curiosity, I suppose. Come on, Kadi, you'd have done the same. A secret underground cavern where you can think and dream and—"

"And spy on people through a termite hole." I can feel myself getting angry.

"I like watching you read. What's wrong with that? You always look so solemn and pretty when you're reading. Sometimes I try to guess what you're reading just by the expression on your face."

"That's weird," I tell him straight. "I'm sorry, Yusuf, that's just creepy."

"It saved your skin this afternoon," he mutters. "As soon as I saw him kick that manuscript, I ran over here to help you. You could at least be grateful, Kadi."

I am grateful, of course. More grateful than he thinks.

Grateful that he left his spy hole when he did.

Grateful for what he doesn't know—that I kissed Ali first.

Ali

We drag the bookcase below the trap door. I clamber up it, breathe a prayer, and jump, relying on the trapdoor's wooden frame to take my weight.

Alhamdulillah! I hold on tight and pedal thin air, breathing heavily.

"Well done, son," says Redbeard.

Three little words, that's all, but they impart peculiar strength. With one explosive biceps curl I pull myself up and through the hole.

Redbeard throws me the flashlight and I shine it around. I am in a stale-smelling bedroom. The mud-brick walls are covered with posters of minstrels and musicians. In a corner stands a brand new ngoni, and here by the trapdoor are the ropes they must have used for hoisting trunks.

I drop a rope for Redbeard, and he climbs up.

A hole has been bashed through the west-facing, mud-brick

wall, in a great hurry by the looks of it. We step out through the jagged hole and find ourselves in the open air. A vast, sandy plain stretches away toward the grass-mat domes of the nomad camps and the dunes beyond.

I shine the flashlight on the sand around my feet, and yes, it's as I thought. A crowd of people were here not long ago, and they were carrying heavy loads.

There are huge tire tracks too, with a well-defined tread. A cattle truck, perhaps.

Redbeard dials a number on his phone.

"Zaarib, I need the Ninjas," he barks. "In fact, I need the whole platoon. Scramble the vehicles. Meet me in the square."

"Shall I go on ahead?" I ask. "I could take the horse."

My master beams and thumps me on the back. "Ride like the wind, Ali. *Don't let them get away.*"

Redbeard hoists me up onto the roof of Kadi's house. I run across it and drop down into the horse's pen beyond.

On a hook on the wall hang the bridle and reins. I make a tutting sound to calm the horse and lift the harness over its head. As for the saddle, I don't have time.

The flashlight is in my mouth, my AK-47 is strapped across my body. I hop onto Marimba's back, and guide him out into the dark, deserted street. I steer him gently down the alleyway between the whitewashed villas and finally emerge onto the plain where Redbeard stands.

"*Allez!*" I cry, and kick my heels, and give the horse his head. He lunges straightaway into a gallop so fierce I have to grab his mane to keep my seat. We fly across the plain beneath the stars, and through the nomad camps and out the other side.

The tracks of the truck lead in a sweeping arc behind the Cemetery of the Three, behind the Sababou vegetable gardens, and on into the dunes. Camel grass and acacia trees flash by on either side. There are no roads here, and no checkpoints either.

Clever Kadija. You know what you are doing, don't you?

But I know what I'm doing too, and this terrain is a stallion's dream. Up a dune, along a ridge, and down, Marimba plows the powdery sand like an avenging djinni. Foam from his mouth flecks my face. I lean down low across his mane and whisper strength into his pricked-back ears.

The tire tracks continue west for about ten miles, then curve toward the south. One thing I know for sure: hooves are faster than wheels on this surface. I am gaining on them with every stride.

Kadi hates her father's horse already. After tonight she'll hate him even more.

Sixteen kilometers farther south, Marimba is nearing the limit of his strength. He is trying to climb another dune, but his head is rolling from side to side and his haunches are starting to sag.

"You can do it, boy," I whisper in his ear.

I cannot, must not, let her escape. If she succeeds in spiriting those manuscripts away, our work today will all have been in vain. Those dangerous books will work their magic even from afar, enthralling desert souls for years to come.

Marimba staggers over the brow of the dune, and what a view unfolds in front of us! A swath of deep, meandering black, and lines of tiny lights, some true, some shimmering.

Of course. Kabara port.

I came here once as a child and watched the trade rafts being loaded up with spices, salt, and strong green tea. I remember the olive-brown water, the cobblestone embankment, and the infinite marsh grass. More than anything, I remember the noise: the hammering of boatwrights, the sawing of salt slabs, the to-ing and fro-ing of porters, and the cries of roving traders.

The smell of water lends the horse one final burst of strength. He lurches down the dune and in amongst the fishing huts, his sweat-slick flanks heaving and shuddering between my knees.

The minstrels back in Goundam have a song about this place.

"Kabara, Kabara,
Where camel meets canoe,
The Gate of the Sahara,
Since time itself began."

Even now, at three o'clock in the morning, the port is a termite mound of activity. Platoons of porters hoist their sacks and crates down to the cobblestone embankment. Fishing canoes and trading rafts jostle for space in the marshy shallows. The reflections of a thousand lamps and flashlights shimmer on the water.

Hundreds of travelers doze on plastic mats or sit in groggy, cross-legged huddles, waiting for their calls to board. I knew that people were fleeing Timbuktu, but I never imagined crowds like these.

The cattle-truck tracks lead down onto a tarmac road and there, annoyingly, I lose them. There are a dozen trucks parked along the road in various stages of loading and unloading, but not a manuscript trunk in sight.

I ride on down to the bank of the river and trot along the rows of bobbing rafts, examining the merchandise. Over here are crates of carrots and cabbages from the Sababou vegetable gardens. Over there are sacks of coal and bundles of salt. I sweep my beam of light across the hurrying porters—more vegetables, more coal, some baskets of salted fish. And then, momentarily, in the beam of my flashlight, the glint of a diamanté veil.

With a metal trunk on top.

I know that veil. It belongs to Kadi's stupid, short-haired girlfriend.

"Aisha!" I shout.

She stops and turns toward me.

"Put down that trunk!" I loom toward her on my horse.

She puts it down.

"Take off your veil!"

She bobs and cowers. "It is forbidden," she says, in a funny voice. "In Timbuktu, females above the age of ten must—"

I don't have time for this. I reach down, snatch her veil away, and shine my flashlight full in her face.

It is not Aisha. It is not even a girl. It is Yusuf, Kadija's skinny cousin, the one who tried to kill me in the vault.

Impaled on the beam of my flashlight, his pupils shrink to tiny dots. He panics, grabs the trunk, and scampers off along the waterfront.

There is no way he can escape, of course. He is on foot with a heavy trunk, and I am on a horse. I spur Marimba into one last trot, draw up beside the fleeing boy, and leap onto his back, slamming him face-first into the mud.

I hear Marimba trotting off, but I don't care. I have my man.

"My nose," moans Yusuf, pinching his nostrils to stem the blood. "I think you've broken it."

"Open the trunk," I tell him. "*Tamba-tamba*. Fast-fast."

"It's padlocked," he says. "I don't have the key."

"Where are the other trunks? Where are you loading them?"

Yusuf squints up at me, still cradling his nose. "Let's do a deal," he whines. "You set my sister, Kamisa, free, I'll lead you to the boat."

"I don't have the authority to free anybody."

"Call your master, then."

180

The manuscripts will get away unless I find them soon. He knows it. I know it. I switch my phone to speakerphone, and make the call.

"Deal," Redbeard says, when I've told him where I am and what is happening. "I'll ring Zaarib and arrange it straightaway. Tell the boy his father will call five minutes from now to confirm the girl's release."

"You've got what you wanted," I say. "Now take me to your boat."

The horse is nowhere to be seen, so we go on foot. Yusuf hoists the trunk onto his head and leads me west along the riverbank.

Five minutes downriver from the port, we arrive at a hidden inlet. Here there is no cobblestone embankment, just a mass of marsh grass sloping down into the river. We wade among the grass, ankle deep in murky water.

"There," whispers Yusuf, pointing.

I see the silhouette of a colossal boat a hundred paces east of where we stand, slumbering low in the water. By the faint light of the moon, I can just make out the lettering: *Compagnie Malienne de Navigation*.

I know the ferry well, as does everyone on this river. For as long as I can remember, this hulking paddle steamer has plied its trade between Gao in the east and Mopti in the west, with Kabara in the middle. From July until January, it rumbles back and forth, its bottom deck stuffed with cargo and its upper decks thronged with people. A few years ago, the steam turbine was replaced by a diesel engine, but they left the massive paddle wheel as a reminder of the olden days.

The ferry is moored by one rope at the bow and another at the stern. A gangplank leads from the grassy shallows onto the deck of the boat. In the middle of the plank stands Kadija, arms folded, feet apart, gazing out across the marshy riverbank.

"What's she waiting for?" I whisper to Yusuf.

"Me," he says. "This is the last trunk."

"Where are the rest?"

"Bottom deck."

Yes, he's telling the truth. I can make out the stacks of metal trunks from here—hundreds of them.

"How many people on board?"

"Just Kadi and the driver."

Just Kadi and the driver. I can finish this on my own.

Yusuf's phone begins to buzz. He takes the call and a grin spreads across his face.

"*Alhamdulillah*," he whispers. "That was my father. Kamisa has been freed!"

"Good."

Good for jihad is what I mean. The very soul of Timbuktu in return for one little girl. Of course my master agreed to the exchange.

"Give me your veil and your outer robe," I say. "And drop your phone in the water."

He does as he is told.

I wave my rifle toward the north. "Go home," I whisper. "And don't make any noise, or I will shoot you in the back."

He turns and starts to wade away, skinnier than ever in his T-shirt and shorts. I watch him every step of the way, and he disappears silently into the night.

As soon as he is gone, I don his outer robe and the diamanté veil, hoist the metal trunk onto my head, and wade toward the ferry. My eyes are fixed on Kadi all the way.

Thirty paces from the gangplank, she sees me coming. I half

expect her to cry out in alarm—I am stronger than her cousin and a little taller—but the robe and veil and manuscript trunk are doing their job, for now.

"You took your time!" she calls to me. "Is that the last one?"

I nod.

"No sign of the Ninjas?"

I shake my head. I am fifteen paces from the gangplank now, and Kadija has gone very still.

Ten paces.

Her posture stiffens, and then she turns on her heel and runs aboard.

She knows.

I lunge forward, splashing through the marsh grass to the foot of the gangplank.

"Crank the engine!" she yells.

Down in the bowels of the boat, a massive diesel engine throbs into life, and the colossal paddle wheel behind the boat begins to turn.

I clatter up the gangplank with the trunk still on my head. The engine growls. The ferry tugs against its mooring ropes, jolting the gangplank so that I lurch and stagger. The trunk slips off my head into the water down below.

Kadija runs to the bow with a machete and severs the mooring rope with a single swipe. The ferry's nose swings out into the river, the gangplank shifts and slides, and now I am down on my hands and knees, crawling up the plank toward the deck.

"More throttle!" cries Kadija, sprinting along the gangway to the sternward mooring rope.

The engine roars, the rope pulls taut, and although I do not see the second swing of the knife I hear a sound like the twang of an enormous kora. The ferry lurches forward. The gangplank slides off the edge of the gunwale and plummets, with me, into the murky water.

I reach out and touch the ferry's hull, but there is nothing to hold on to and it slides away from me, accelerating toward the middle of the river.

"Good-bye, Ali!" Kadija calls. "I love you!"

Insolent, sarcastic, godless girl! She thinks she's won. She thinks I'll hang my head in shame and wade on up to solid land.

She's wrong. Water holds no terror for me, or for any son of Goundam. As a child I used to swim in Lake Télé every day, playing waterdog and eel tag with my friends. Now that I am a man, it's time to play eel tag for real. I tear the veil from my face, kick the flip-flops off my feet, and start to swim.

When I came to Kabara as a child, I witnessed something extraordinary. I saw a tigerfish leap out of the river and catch a bronze-winged mannikin in flight.

Tonight, *inshallah*, that tigerfish is me. My eyes are good. My fins are powerful. My jaws are razor sharp. My body lifts out of the water, I take a gulp of air, my shoulders swing forward like twin pistons, and my arms plunge down into the roiling river. Up and down, up and down, I power through the ferry's seething wake.

When the ferry reaches the middle of the river, the driver opens the throttle as far as it will go. The paddle wheel rotates faster and faster, churning the river into boiling ink.

I am swimming downriver with the current but the ferry is too fast. My arms are burning, my shoulder blades tightening, and the boat is a shrinking silhouette against the moonlit sky.

I swim on all the same.

I swim on because I am a tigerfish and my prey is still in sight.

I swim on because the treasure aboard that boat belongs to Timbuktu, and Timbuktu belongs to us.

I swim on because no paddle wheel in the world can outpropel a warrior of God.

I swim on because I know this stretch of river. Just beneath the surface, mudflats lurk.

At long last, I hear ahead of me the sounds I have been longing for: a watery slap, a grinding of gravel and gears, a mechanical whine, and a clunk. And then no sound at all, apart from the splash of my own arms in the water and the whirr of insects on the riverbank.

My strength is spent, my calves are cramping, my fingers are clawed with cold, but my heart rejoices. The ferry has run aground.

Spurred on by hope of victory, I press on through the dark until I reach the ferry. I grab the severed mooring rope and haul myself over the gunwale. *Alhamdulillah!* I lie on my side on the edge of the cargo deck, panting and dry-retching and praising God, sodden clothes clinging to my body.

Kadija is standing over me with the knife she used to cut the mooring ropes. She could kill me right now if she wanted to. She won't, of course. I know her, and she won't.

"*Foofo,*" I pant.

"*Foofo,*" she says.

Another minute passes, and then I gesture toward the stacks of manuscript trunks. "Smuggling national treasures is against the law."

"Only if they leave the country," she replies. "There is nothing illegal about moving private property within Mali's borders."

I can think of a hundred clever retorts, but I am much too out of breath to carry on talking. I sit up and reach for my toes to try to ease the cramping in my calves. The river is still and silent, and the full moon hangs low in the west, glinting on Kadija's knife.

Hurrying footsteps sound from the engine room below, and a moment later a man appears behind Kadija. It is Tijani Traoré, the swarthy ferryman from Niafunke. Everybody knows Tijani. He has driven the ferry for more than thirty years.

I get to my feet and shrug the rifle off my back. AK-47s work perfectly even when they're waterlogged.

"Kadi, throw the knife overboard," I say.

She does as she is told, swinging her arm to lob the machete high into the air. It turns over and over and lands in the river with a plop.

"Now listen, both of you," I say. "These manuscripts of yours are not good for Timbuktu. Apart from that one Al-Fatiha, what use are they? Childish fairy tales, senseless superstitions, outdated astronomy, irrelevant laws, the ramblings of senile, old men. Half of them are unreadable, anyway. The termites have seen to that."

Kadija shrugs. "If a man can't see the sun at noon, don't try to show him."

The ferryman sniggers at the proverb.

"Shut up!" I shout at him, pointing the muzzle of my gun at his midriff. "I'm not the blind one, Traoré, you are! You should have known that the river from here to Gao is full of mudflats. If you had gone west toward Mopti, you would have avoided the mudflats, and I would have been swimming against the current. I could never have caught up with you."

"True, very true."

"And Mopti is still government controlled, so you would have been safe there, whereas Gao—" I break off, amazed at their stupidity.

"Whereas Gao is controlled by Al Qaeda," says the ferryman. "He's right, Kadija. Even if we had reached Gao, we would not have lasted five minutes."

186

"This is your fault, Tijani!" cries Kadija. "You told me you knew the river like your own arm."

"It's not my fault, it's yours!" the ferryman yells back. "It was you who insisted that your cousin wear that stupid veil. Those diamanté panels stand out a mile, even in the dark. You know they do! If he hadn't worn that veil, none of this would have happened!"

They are pretending to argue, but their teeth are shining in the moonlight. They are grinning their heads off.

Why are they so happy? What have I missed?

The morning prayer call blares from the minaret of a faraway mosque. I grasp my rifle in both hands and force my tired brain to think. Why head downriver toward Gao, when they knew it wasn't deep enough? Why strand themselves deliberately? And why choose such a conspicuous veil? It's almost like they *wanted* me to find Yusuf.

A dreadful thought occurs to me. I stumble to my feet. "Give me the keys, Kadija!" I cry. "Give me the keys to the padlocks!"

"What padlocks? The trunks aren't locked."

My heart is galloping as I walk to the manuscript stacks. The dark river pulsates at the edges of my vision. She's right—there are no padlocks. I lift down a trunk from the nearest stack, drag it into the moonlight, lift the lid.

Carrots.

I open another.

Cabbages.

There is charcoal in the third and fourth, and salt in the fifth.

"Where are they?" I cry. "Kadija, where are the manuscripts?"

"Heading west." She smiles. "Like you just said, Mopti is definitely the best place for them."

I think of the rafts at Kabara, and the porters with their bundles, crates, and sacks. Bundles of salt tablets with manuscripts interspersed. Crates of manuscripts with vegetables on top. Sacks of manuscripts with coal on top. *They have smuggled twelve thousand manuscripts out of Timbuktu right under my nose.*

I take my waterlogged phone out of my pocket and try to switch it on. It's dead, of course.

"Your phones," I tell them. "Give me your phones right now."

Kadija and the ferryman exchange a glance, take out their phones, and lob them in the river.

"No!" I shout.

These last two weeks I have been shot by Kadija's musket, beaten up by her friends, lashed by Muhammad Zaarib, tripped up on the vault stairs, and mocked and lied to more times than I can count, but this is the greatest humiliation of them all. This will be talked about in Timbuktu for years to come. For centuries, perhaps.

"I broke your cousin's nose," I tell her. It is small comfort, but it is all I have.

Kadija shrugs. "I will kiss it better for him."

I stand there impotent, clicking my knuckles. The ferryman sits down on a trunk of cabbages and folds his arms. It is too dark to see his expression, but I can feel his contempt. It comes at me in waves, like the lapping of the river on the ferry's hull.

Kadi walks up close to me, close enough to speak without being overheard.

"Abdullai," she whispers, looking up at me. "I'm sorry for pretending you attacked me. When my cousin turned up, I got scared. If my parents found out what really happened, they would never let me be a Guardian."

I turn my back on her, dig the butt of my rifle into my right shoulder, and fire thirty rounds into the air on full automatic.

"Master!" I yell. "I'm here! Come quickly, master!"

An hour later, with the sky beginning to lighten in the east, Redbeard arrives in a fishing boat with an outboard motor. Jabir and Hamza are with him.

"Well done, Ali Konana!" he cries, climbing up and hauling himself over the rail. "You've caught them red-handed."

"No," I mutter miserably. "They've tricked us, master."

I show him the trunks of vegetables and he glowers at them silently, shaking his head as if trying to wake from a nightmare. Redbeard is not used to losing. He doesn't know how.

At last, he finds his voice. "Stupid boy," he hisses, and it hurts.

"Sorry, master."

"These are the tricksters, are they?" Redbeard gestures at Kadi and the ferryman. "What are their names?"

I tell him.

Redbeard walks up close to them and folds his arms. "Well done, Ali Konana," he says. "You've caught them red-handed."

"No, master, I told you—"

"Kadija Diallo and Tijani Traoré," says Redbeard. "You are both under arrest."

Kadi giggles. "For what? For smuggling cabbages?"

"No," says Redbeard slowly. "For fornication."

Surely not. He must be joking.

But Kadi is no longer giggling. "On what evidence?"

"You know very well, Kadija. A young unmarried girl cavorting alone with a ferryman in the middle of the Niger River before the call to prayer has even sounded from the mosque?"

"We weren't cavorting!"

"Let Al-Qadi Zaarib be the judge of that."

"He's not a *qadi*!" She stamps her foot. "And he hates women. You know he does. I won't have a chance."

"No," says Redbeard, considering her point. "No, I suppose you won't."

Kadija slumps down on a metal trunk and puts her face in her hands.

"Hamza, start the motor!" calls Redbeard. "Ali, guard the prisoners!"

I stand over Kadi with my gun, and the scent of oleander makes me want to cry.

"Abdullai," she whispers. "Are you going to let them punish me for a lie?"

"I have no choice."

"The real you has a choice," she whispers. "The real you loves soccer and music and—"

"And what?"

"And me."

☾

We bundle our prisoners into the boat and motor back toward Kabara. The sun is rising in the east. Fat-necked jacana birds tiptoe across water lilies. Silhouetted fishermen stand tall in dugout canoes, casting their nets to fall in perfect circles on the river's surface.

Hamza is more cheerful than I have ever seen him. "In the name of God," he keeps saying, "this night will be numbered among the most glorious raiding expeditions in Muslim history."

"Shut up," I tell him.

Shutting up is the last thing on his mind. "From this night on," he declares, "the troubadours of Timbuktu will no longer speak of Nedj, where Zayd Haritha seized a hundred thousand dirhams of gold. They will speak no longer of the thousand silver camels of Al-Is, or the fifty thousand dinars at the oasis of Badr. No, they will speak of Kabara, where the great Ali

Konana seized"—he pauses for effect—"five thousand shining cabbages!"

☾

Back in Timbuktu, Muhammad Zaarib meets us at the entrance to the police station.

"Fornication on a ferry," he says, rubbing his hands. "Were there witnesses?"

"Me," says Redbeard, "and Ali Konana here."

"They are lying!" Kadi shouts. "They're upset because I smuggled my manuscripts out of Timbuktu and made them look stupid."

Zaarib doesn't even look at her. "One hundred lashes," he says. "That's a first for Timbuktu. Put her in the cell, and we will punish her this afternoon, *inshallah*."

One hundred lashes. They're actually going ahead with this. I didn't say anything on the ferry because I assumed my master would change his mind as soon as he calmed down. Surely he knows as well as I do that false accusation is the worst kind of lie.

"What about the ferryman?" Redbeard is saying. "Should we lash him too?"

"We can't have them sharing a cell," says Zaarib. "It would be improper. Let him go with a warning, just this once."

"You heard him, Tijani Traoré," says Redbeard. "Off you go."

The swarthy ferryman blinks and shakes his head, but he does not dispute the ruling. Like a sleepwalker he moves away stiff-legged into Independence Square.

"Tell Mama I'm here!" Kadija shouts at his retreating back. "Tell her the charges are false!"

"God and I will be the judge of that," says Zaarib.

God and I. The phrase trips off his tongue so easily.

A strange sensation comes over me. I am out of my body, floating in a haze of heat above the shimmering square. I see scrubby acacia trees, a headless djinni atop a horse, and a cluster of humans on the steps of a police station. Five black turbans and one black veil, and swirling within those swaths of black are anger, pride, dismay, and dread. Unholy, all of it.

Redbeard's voice brings me harshly back to ground. "Tell me, Ali Konana, when did you last sleep?"

"I don't know. The day before yesterday, I think."

"That's why you look so terrible," says Redbeard. "Let's go back to camp."

I walk at my master's side. The silence between us is heavy and sullen. Words from the Book are pounding in my head: *Those who malign believing men and believing women undeservedly, they bear the guilt of slander and manifest sin.*

Near the gate of our camp, my master turns to me and scowls. "War is deceit," he snaps. "Not my words. The Prophet's."

I say nothing. I long to talk to Omar, or even to my father back in Goundam. He is spiritually obtuse, of course, but I wouldn't mind hearing his voice.

As we enter through the gates of the camp, Redbeard takes a folded piece of paper from the pocket of his outer robe, glances at it briefly, and drops it into the metal barrel that we use for burnable rubbish.

"Sleep well," he says to me, and hurries off into his private quarters.

I stay beside the barrel. As soon as my master is gone, I reach inside and pluck the paper out. *Yes, just what I thought.* It's the mislaid manuscript we found behind that bookcase in the vault.

Beside the sorry remains of Tamba-Tamba's tomb, I sit on my mat to examine the manuscript. The single page is crammed with fine calligraphy, with a rust-brown footnote scrawled beneath. The footnote reads:

Written in Ephesus, copied in Damascus, sold to the Sultan Al-Mansur of Marrakesh, and brought to Timbuktu by Ahmad Baba on his return from exile.

My shoulders and back are throbbing painfully. I'll read the manuscript, and then I'll try to sleep.

Manuscript 9,576: the tarikh of Isa ibn Maryam

Isa ibn Maryam was a prophet great in word and deed. Yahya of Ephesus recorded many of the prophet's miracles and wise judgments.

One morning, Isa ibn Maryam was preaching in the temple courts, when the teachers of the law brought in a woman caught in adultery. They stood her in front of everyone and said to Isa, "Teacher, this woman was caught in the act of adultery. The Prophet Musa commanded us to stone such women to death. What do you say?"

Isa ibn Maryam bent down and wrote in the sand with his finger. When they kept on questioning him, he straightened up and said to them, "Let any one of you who is without sin be the first to throw a stone at her." Again he stooped and wrote in the sand.

At this, those who heard began to go away one at a time, the older ones first and then the younger ones. Finally, only Isa was left, with the woman still standing there.

Isa straightened up and asked her, "Woman, where are they? Has no one condemned you?"

"No one, master," she said.

"Then neither do I condemn you," Isa said. "Go now and leave your life of sin."

May the blessing of Isa ibn Maryam be upon us.

Kadija

A hundred lashes. This very afternoon. *A hundred lashes.*

I am alone and staring at the four walls of my cell. It is drab and windowless, a dismal scene. The only things in the cell are this short wooden bench I'm sitting on, and the stinking bucket in the corner.

A hundred lashes. My stomach heaves every time I think about it.

Mama came to see me earlier on. I spent ten minutes crying on her neck, and then she had to go.

She tried to give me strength, of course. She told me Baba is out of the cleaning cupboard and in a proper ward. And she got a call from Aisha on the manuscript flotilla. They are well out of the danger zone and on their way to Mopti.

When Mama was here, my fears withdrew, but now that she's gone they crowd back with a vengeance.

A hundred lashes. If I had not seen what twenty lashes does to a girl, I might not be so terrified. But I have, and I am. Faint, cold fear is thrilling through my veins.

Hasbi rabijal Allah. Hasbi rabijal Allah. Hasbi rabijal Allah.

It's no use. Not even *dhikr* can repel the terror.

She gave me clothes, Mama did, and a copy of the Book, and a vial of oleander perfume sewn into the hem of a veil. I thought she would refuse me the perfume, but she didn't. Dear Mama. She has no idea what I need it for.

I run my hand over the bottle's neck and hips, uncork it, run my finger round the rim. There is peace in this bottle, and freedom, and an end to pain.

I am crying now. Madness is coming on me and there is nothing I can do. I feel it invading, capturing, occupying me.

"Be careful with that perfume of yours," Uncle Abdel used to tell me. Uncle Abdel owns an Ahmad Baba treatise on the subject of oleander, and he has told me what it can do to a person.

At first, of course, you will feel nothing out of the ordinary, but then your heart will start to speed up. After five minutes it will be pounding in your chest like the hooves of a cantering horse. Your skin will go waxy. Your fingers and toes will grow cold. After fifteen minutes you will begin to shake violently like an old woman at a djinni possession ceremony. And after thirty minutes you will be dead.

It is a wondrous thing, oleander extract. Dab a little on your wrists and neck and breasts and it transports your mind to the luscious rose gardens of Paradise itself. Drink it, and it takes your body there.

A Yamaha motorbike roars into earshot, and suddenly I hear the voice of Uncle Abdel at the door of the police station. He is arguing with the jailer, demanding to come in. Mama told him that I asked for perfume. He is afraid I might hurt myself.

Too right I might.

Blinking through tears, I carry the wooden bench to the door of my cell, and stand it on end, jamming the door handle so that it will not budge a millimeter. Nothing short of a grenade could open that door now.

It's good of Uncle Abdel to worry, but he is too late. He does not understand. He has never felt this darkness, or this depth of fear.

I raise the bottle to my lips.

What's that?

On the bottom of the bench, someone has scratched five words.

Ko jemma boni fu, weetan.

Underneath the proverb is a single letter *K*.

Kamisa.

My cheerful, beautiful young cousin spent three days and three nights in this very cell, battling demons of her own.

Ko jemma boni fu, weetan. Even if the night is bad, morning will come.

I hurl the vial at the far wall of my cell. I cannot see for tears, but I hear the clay vial shatter into a million shards, and oh, the fragrance! The fragrance! The fragrance!

٭

Late afternoon prayer is finished, and though there is no window in my cell, I can hear the people gathering in Independence Square. They are coming to tut and to stare and to shake their heads in sorrow. Coming to see whether a fifteen-year-old girl can survive a hundred lashes, and to grieve for Timbuktu.

I arrange my hair, put my veil on, and slide the bench out from under the door handle. If I resist them now, I will only make it worse.

A sudden hush comes over the crowd, and I hear the hum of an approaching Land Cruiser. It stops, the engine cuts, and car doors slam.

"The city of Timbuktu is built on Islam and only Islamic law applies in it. Bring out the evildoer!"

Evildoer. That's me.

A key clicks in the lock and the door opens. My jailer steps aside to let me pass, then follows me along the silent corridor toward the light. There is the crowd, six deep around the edges of the square, men on one side and women on the other. So many faces I know and love, and each one etched with pity. Five turbaned boys with AK-47s are perching on the back of the Land Cruiser trailer. Muhammad Zaarib is somewhere nearby, with a whip. If I look at him I will collapse, I know I will.

"Kadija Diallo," calls Redbeard through a megaphone. "Fornication. One hundred lashes."

The crowd gasps.

One hundred. They are actually going to do it.

My jailer kneels me down gently on the warm sand, and I hear Zaarib's footsteps behind me. Try as I might I can't stop myself shivering.

Ya Rabbu rham. Lord, have mercy on me.

For one insane moment I am thrilled to be the center of attention, with the whole of Timbuktu looking at me.

Then the first lash falls across my back.

The thrill is gone and all that's left is pain. I just have time to suck in a mouthful of air before the second lash falls. It hurts even more than the first one, more than I could have believed possible. I should have drunk the perfume when I had the chance.

"Shame on you, you brutes!" shrieks a woman in the front row.

Three. I'm not brave like Halimatu or Ramata. I live in a nice villa and I sing songs and wear perfume and read books, but I'm no good at pain. Aisha used to laugh at me and call me soft. *Sweet and soft, like fresh-baked bread.*

Four. Groans from the crowd, and anger.

I reach down, pick up a handful of sand, and squeeze it in my palm. What worked for Ramata can work for me as well. *As soon as the sand turns to oil, my dear, then you can cry out.*

It doesn't work for me. The fifth lash lands, my hands fly open into startled claws, and all the sand falls out.

It didn't turn to oil—it never does—but I will cry out anyway. I will cry out louder than a megaphone, louder than a Kalashnikov rifle, louder than the desert's singing dunes. I will cry out more savagely than any girl has ever cried, and the grim facades of Independence Square will crumble into dust. Saharan fennecs will plug their furry ears, and every mosque in Timbuktu will melt.

Ali

I never wanted this. It's hideous. I perch on the edge of the Land Cruiser trailer, my stomach heaving.

On the fourth lash she reaches down and scoops up a palmful of sand. On the fifth lash she drops it with a whimper.

This is going to kill her. I know that now without a trace of doubt.

On the sixth lash she lifts her head and straightens her back, and through the veil comes a cry so loud it makes me jump.

"Alla La Ke!"

Zaarib's whip arm stops. The crowd goes silent. They know the song, and so do I. I used to play it on the flute.

"Alla La Ke!"

Zaarib scowls and swings his arm a seventh time and Kadi is sobbing fiercely through her veil, and then she lifts her head and sings again.

"Alla La Ke!"

Once upon a time in the land of Tumana there lived two princes. *Eight.* When the chieftaincy was being passed down, one prince stole it from the other and banished him from Tumana. *Nine.* Eventually the rightful heir returned and had the chieftaincy given to him. *Ten.*

"Alla La Ke!"

Eleven. Instead of taking revenge on his brother, the new king forgave him all that he had done.

"Alla La Ke!" she sings, and pain lends power to her voice.

I look up at the black standard flying from the roof of the town hall. Someone should silence her, or that flag will rend itself from top to bottom.

Zaarib is doing his best, grunting with the exertion of each lash. "Shut up," he hisses. "Shut up, shut up!"

Twelve. You cannot force God's hand. *Thirteen.* Be patient, and the reign of the dark prince will pass. *Fourteen.* Hold fast, people. A dark regime cannot last.

She sang this song at her friend's wedding. That night I lurked at the back of the crowd disguised in beggar's clothes, tormented by the beauty of her singing and the wrongness of it. This afternoon I sit up front with my AK-47, tormented by the beauty of her singing and the rightness of it.

"Alla La Ke!"

That wasn't her. That was a boy's voice.

I turn toward the men's side of the square. A boy in dark glasses has stepped forward out of line, as bold as a balaphone.

"Alla La Ke!" he sings.

A girl in a pink veil on the other side of the square steps forward. Her hands are shaking but her voice is strong and pure.

"Alla La Ke!" she sings.

An old man steps forward too. He is leaning heavily on his stick, and his beard is as white as the Prophet Ibrahim's.

"Alla La Ke!" His voice is quavery, discordant, but it imparts strange courage to his neighbors.

"*Alla La Ke! Alla La Ke!*" All over the crowd now, people are singing.

Redbeard turns to me and the other Ninjas. "Control them," he mouths.

Hamza and the others spread out around the square. They storm and scold and jab their rifles into people's chests, but the singing continues, swelling to a crescendo in the rose-red square.

I hop down from the trailer and stoop in the shadow of the truck.

Isa ibn Maryam bent down and wrote in the sand with his finger. When they kept on questioning him, he straightened up and said to them, "Let any one of you who is without sin be the first to throw a stone at her." Again he stooped and wrote in the sand.

I stretch out my finger and write. *In the name of God, the Compassionate and Merciful.*

As I write the holy words, a flicker of movement catches my eye. A small, black scorpion is scuttling toward me in the shadow of the truck. It looks just like the one that Redbeard killed last night.

Perhaps, after all, it's not too late.

When you pick up a scorpion, confidence is the thing. You have to reach out smoothly and grasp it by the sting in one quick motion. Don't hesitate. Just do it.

Adrenaline clears my mind and hones my reactions. I reach out, pinch the scorpion's sting, and lift it up. It squirms in midair, furious.

I walk round behind Redbeard and drop it down the back of his neck. He flinches and reaches over his shoulder to pat his back. The scorpion delivers its sting.

The sting won't kill him: I know that much. I just need to get his gun.

Redbeard's reactions are lightning quick. He shrugs his AK-47 off his shoulder, grasps his robe by the corners, whips it off over his head, and launches into a bare-chested dance, trying to locate his attacker. He whirls and stomps like the pilgrims at the tomb of Sidi Ahmed.

Nervous laughter mingles with the singing in the crowd.

I pick up Redbeard's gun and sling it across my body. Now I have two.

Zaarib has not noticed his comrade dancing. He is concentrating on the lash. *Twenty-one. Twenty-two. Twenty-three.* I wait until the whip is at its highest point, then grab the handle tight with my left hand.

As Zaarib turns to look at me, I hit out hard with the heel of my right hand, hitting him in the forehead and following through until my arm is perfectly straight.

The fake *qadi* falls backwards unconscious on the sand.

A heel strike to the forehead is a useful weapon, Redbeard always says. It rocks your opponent's brain inside the skull and lays him out for half an hour or more.

In the name of God, the Compassionate and Merciful, I grab Kadi's wrist and the knot of her wraparound skirt and drape her across my shoulders like a lamb.

At last, Redbeard has realized what is going on. His finger moves for the trigger of his AK-47.

And finds nothing there but his own protruding navel.

In the name of God, the Compassionate and Merciful, I kick off my flip-flops and run.

The crowd parts to let me through and closes up after me. I am running up Toumani Avenue, keeping close to the ornate mud-brick wall on my right. As I arrive at the Sidi Yahya Mosque, I hear a voice behind me.

"Stop right there, Konana!"

Hamza.

There is no way I can outrun him, not with Kadi on my back. The main front doors of the compound are closed and bolted from inside.

"Imam Cissé!" I call. "Open up."

No answer.

"Stop!" shouts Hamza again. "Don't think I won't kill you, Konana!"

The mosque is set into the compound wall, and its sloping sides are decorated with bundles of horizontal rodier palm. Once a year, on Timbuktu Replastering Day, these bristles serve as scaffolding. The boys of Timbuktu climb round from rung to rung and slap new mud onto the ancient walls.

"Hold on tight," I whisper to Kadi, and I hop up onto the rung nearest the door. Higher and higher I climb, until I am level with the top of the wall.

A burst of gunfire crackles from below, pulverizing the wall around my head.

I stop climbing.

"It was your fault, Konana!" shouts Hamza. "If you had not fallen off that rope, my brother would still be here!"

"I know!" I shout. "I'm sorry, Hamza."

"Not good enough!" he yells. "It should have been you on the top of that wall, Konana. It should have been you the sentry shot!"

"I'm sorry," I say again, and it's the truth.

"Throw me both those guns, Konana. And if you put your fingers anywhere near a trigger, I will shoot you both."

I let the AK-47s fall. They clatter on the sand.

"Good," says Hamza. "Now drop the girl, as well."

He's mad, I think. His grief and guilt has sent him mad.

"Drop the girl," he repeats slowly, "or I will kill you both."

"If I drop her from this height, she'll break her bones. You know she will."

"And if you don't," drawls Hamza, "she will be shot."

"She's innocent," I say. "Redbeard lied about last night. This girl's done nothing wrong."

"The sentence has been passed, Konana. Can't undo it now!"

He's right, of course, but here's the thing: I'm tired of sharia. I'm tired of lashing and being lashed. I'm tired of Timbuktu. I want to go home.

Hamza raises his gun to shoot. "*Salaam alaikum,* Konana," he says. "Peace be with you."

I feel a slender hand plunge into the pocket of my robe and out again. It takes a second for me to realize what Kadi is doing.

Hamza squints, then frowns as he spots an object falling toward him. He sees it land and roll between his feet—a hand grenade!

The fisherboy knows he has no more than three seconds till detonation. He sprints ten paces and throws himself to the ground, burying his head between his elbows.

The deadly fruit lies motionless on the sand.

Kadi, you genius. You remembered my lucky grenade.

Five seconds are all it takes to pick my way across the rodier rungs onto the shaded, eastern buttress of the mosque.

Hamza is up and on his feet again, but by the time his furious gunfire strafes the northern wall, Kadi and I are out of his line of fire and clambering down into the courtyard of the mosque.

That crazy heaven-blessed grenade has saved my life a second time, but we are still in danger. I can hear Hamza on the other side of the wall, grunting and cursing as he scrabbles up the rodier sticks.

Tethered to a pillar in a corner of the courtyard stands Imam Cissé's chestnut stallion. I lay Kadija across its back and fumble with the knot round its fetlock.

"Please, no," Kadija groans. "You know I hate horses."

"I'm sorry," I tell her. "It's not for long."

Kadija

We canter out the south gate of the mosque and into the mazelike streets of Timbuktu's old town. Left and right, and right again, we ride the dusty streets, and the sounds of gunfire and shouting recede into the distance. My rescuer handles the stallion well, taking the straights at Harmattan speed but treading cautiously around blind corners. My back is slick with blood, my face with tears. But I'm alive, and one day I may even laugh again.

We pass the Tamasheq charcoal stalls and the Well of Old Buktu. We pass the house of the explorer Heinrich Barth, the bakery, and the potters' yard. We canter under the balanites trees to the plain where the Timbuktu butchers dance.

The sun dips below the mud-brick roofs, and darkness comes upon us like a friend. The stallion slows to a stately walk, and we are out of the city at last, traveling east across a sandy plain. One day I will return to Timbuktu, but for now my place is with my manuscripts.

"You must be thirsty," my rescuer says. "There's a natural spring in those dunes over there, that only we shepherds know about. And maybe we'll find a hollow baobab tree and some honey for your wounds."

I close my eyes and adjust my breathing to the gentle rise and fall of the chestnut stallion's hooves.

"Ali, please," I murmur. "Take me to Mopti."

"Whatever you say," he says. "But stop calling me Ali. My name is Abdullai."

Afterword

Thank you for choosing to read *Blood and Ink*. I do hope you enjoyed it.

This book is based on real events in Timbuktu in 2012. As you know, historical fiction is a tricky genre. How true should you remain to the actual events? How much should you embellish or invent?

All the characters in *Blood and Ink* are entirely fabricated, with the exception of Redbeard (also known as Omar Ould Hamaha, or as Akka), whose colorful history and equally colorful goatee beard ensured his appearance in the story. At the time of writing, he was still at large with a three-million-dollar reward on his head. Although he is now believed to have been killed in French air strikes.

At the heart of this novel are the cultural and religious differences between the moderate Sufi Muslims of Timbuktu and the hard-line Defenders of Faith. There are many militant Islamist groups in the Sahara desert. One is called AQIM (Al Qaeda in the Islamic Mahgreb). Another is called "Defenders of Faith" (Arabic: *Ansar Dine*). They hate the West and its allies, including the government of Mali, and they long for a strict form of Muslim law to be imposed across West Africa. I have described these two groups as best I can through the eyes of Kadija and Ali.

It is true that the invasion of Timbuktu was accomplished by

Tuareg rebels, with only a little help from the Defenders. The Tuaregs are an ethnic group in West Africa. The men are sometimes called "the lords of the Sahara." They wear indigo turbans and ride camels through the desert, buying and selling salt. The Tuaregs live in Mali and other West African countries, but they have always longed to have a country of their own, right in the middle of the Sahara desert. This imagined homeland, Azawad, will be at least the size of Spain, and its three main cities will be Kidal, Gao, and Timbuktu.

The betrayal of the Tuaregs by the Defenders of Faith happened more or less as described. They were given two hours to leave town.

The rules of the new regime (the list of crimes incurring lashes) are authentic. The ban on music included musical ringtones. Many of the key moments in the plot are based on real events, including the destruction of the bars and nightclubs, the anti-veil protest by the women of Timbuktu, and the smuggling operation in which Timbuktu manuscripts were hidden beneath crates of vegetables and loaded into canoes. The smuggling lasted several weeks, though. It did not happen all in one night.

The occupation of Timbuktu lasted for nine months, after which the city was liberated by French and Malian forces. *Ansar Dine* fled into the desert, setting fire to the Ahmad Baba Library on their way out of the city. Few manuscripts were destroyed thanks to the success of the Guardians' smuggling operation. Sporadic terrorist attacks continue in the region, but at the time of writing, the citizens of Timbuktu remain free and defiant. In 2013 they elected the Honorable Madame Maïga Aziza Mint Mohamed, their first-ever female politician.

All the legends of the saints of Timbuktu are authentic, but I have retold them in my own words. When the tombs of the saints were destroyed by the Defenders of Faith, local and international outrage was considerable.

I have never visited Timbuktu, but I have taken pains to ensure that the geography of Timbuktu is correct. I moved the Ahmad Baba Library to the top of Askia Street, but I have left everything else in its proper place.

It is true that there was a stampede outside the Djinguereber Mosque during the feast of Mouloud in 2010. Twenty-six people were crushed to death. Half of them were children.

The Door of Heaven was a real door in the Sidi Yahya Mosque. It was broken down by the Defenders, and the imam of the mosque was offered fifty-thousand francs for its repair. He refused the money.

It is true that the children of some Guardians in Timbuktu take an oath at the age of seventeen to protect the manuscripts in their care.

Ahmad Baba (1556–1627) was the greatest scholar in the history of Timbuktu. That phrase about the ink of the scholars weighing more than the blood of the martyrs is original to him.

John 8, the story of Jesus's response to a woman caught in adultery, is a manuscript fragment that was not originally part of the Gospel of John. I have imagined an Arabic translation of this fragment being brought to Timbuktu by Ahmad Baba in the early seventeenth century, via Damascus and Marrakesh. It is true that manuscripts made their way to Timbuktu from all over the world, but I do not know for sure that this fragment was among them.

The Russian AK-47 assault rifle is used in conflicts all over the world. Its inventor, Mikhail Kalashnikov, died in December 2013. Shortly before his death, he wrote a long letter describing his "spiritual pain" over the many deaths it caused, and asking whether he was to blame for those deaths. "The longer I live," he wrote, "the more this question drills itself into my brain and the more I wonder why the Lord allowed man to have the devilish desires of envy, greed, and aggression."

Acknowledgments

Thank you to Sarah Pakenham, who first directed my attention to Naveena Kottoor's BBC World Service article "How Timbuktu's manuscripts were smuggled to safety," the seed from which this story grew. And because a novelist relies on the generosity and insight of others, my thanks are due also to Dr. Mohammed Mathee, Shindouk Ould Najim, Miranda Dodd, Dr. John Hunwick, Marc and Helen Gallagher, Keith Smith, Andy James, Carolyn Reid, Megan Kerr, editors Monica Perez, Charlie Sheppard, and Chloe Sackur, agent extraordinaire Julia Churchill, and (as always) my ingenious wife, Charlie.